'I've got a job for you. One that's needed doing for a good long while—too long.'

'I warn you, I'm a stubborn, autocratic PA.' Laura smiled.

'Just what I need.' Cal grinned, ushering her into the house. 'I've had things all my own way for far too long.'

Laura was stunned at the chaos. He worked in total disorder. After the neat buildings of the ranch and the smooth running of everything, his office came as a shock. She just stood and looked around in bewilderment.

'Everyone to his own trade,' she said brightly. 'You deal with the ranch and I'll deal with the paperwork.'

'You'll stay?' He looked stunned at her acceptance.

'How could I refuse?'

Patricia Wilson was born in Yorkshire and lived there until she married and had four children. She loves travelling and has lived in Singapore, Africa and Spain. She had always wanted to be a writer, but a growing family and career as a teacher left her with little time to pursue her interest. With the encouragement of her family she gave up teaching in order to concentrate on writing and her other interests of music and painting.

HIS UNEXPECTED PROPOSAL
marks the welcome return of Patricia Wilson to the Tender Romance™ series. Her warm, involving novels have delighted millions of readers around the world.

CHAPTER ONE

As THEY parked the car and walked along to the solicitor's office, Laura was thankful for the breeze blowing against her arms and legs. It wasn't hot but it was better than the rain. She could wear a summer dress, let the wind blow in her hair and allow her spirits to lift.

She was aware that her brother walked beside her, aware of his silence and she knew his mind was following the same track as her own. They had just been to see the place where their father was buried and Laura had been unable to mourn at all.

They hadn't known him. He had left them without a backward glance when they were children. He had not even informed them he'd been back in England. The only reason she knew he was buried had been a brief letter from the solicitor.

It was impossible to feel pity, impossible to feel anything. Tony had been a baby when their father had walked out of their lives but Laura had been eight years old and could still remember the hurt, the tears. She remembered the hugs too and his promise to come back with enough money to make them rich for life.

She hadn't wanted money. She'd only wanted her father. Neither had ever been forthcoming. The letters had soon stopped and finally the memory of the laughing, cheerful man had faded into wistful fancies. Her mother had known the type of person she'd married and had never ceased to mention it. He'd been a dreamer with schemes that had never come to fruition.

Well, they were both dead. Her mother had died over six months ago and Laura had taken on the task of finishing off the raising of her seventeen-year-old brother.

It wasn't much of a task; they got on well together. She shot a quick glance at him. He was taller than she was now and so very clever, but he needed her just as much as he had always needed her. Their mother's constant bitterness had left him anxious, unsure of himself.

The past year had been difficult with their mother's illness and finally her death. Now there were more problems to sort out. She had to calculate how they were going to manage.

'Can you remember what he looked like?' Tony sounded depressed and Laura came out of her schemes and plans.

'Who?'

'Dad. I don't remember him at all.'

'You were only a baby.' She slid her arm into his. 'Yes, I vaguely remember. But really all I'm sure of is that he was always laughing.'

'You must be like him, then.'

Laura certainly hoped not. One dreamer per family was quite enough. She laughed to keep her spirits up in difficult circumstances.

She gave Tony a considering look. 'As far as I remember, you've got his face and his colouring.' She knew that because her mother had remarked about it frequently—with a good deal of foreboding.

'Have I?' Tony cheered up considerably. 'So you've got the memories and I've got the hair. I wonder where you got your colouring?' He gave a flick to her silver-blonde hair. 'Mum didn't have fair hair.'

Laura leaned close to whisper mysteriously, 'Viking ancestors.'

Tony grinned. 'Pity they only left you the hair. We could

have made use of a bit of their plundering. I know you're worrying about how we're going to manage.'

'I am not,' Laura lied reassuringly, not at all certain he believed her. 'Get a move on. We've got an appointment with the solicitor and it's almost time.'

'What do you think Dad left us? Let's hope it wasn't his debts.'

He was anxious again. In many ways they had both suffered from their mother's angry resentment. She had encouraged them to be troubled but Laura had always found it easier to be upbeat about things.

'Dad might have found his Eldorado and left it all to us. There might be a gold mine or a palace or some lost kingdom where he was king.' She walked briskly, the wind blowing her hair like a bright pennant.

Tony burst into laughter. 'You sound like Mum's tales of him. I always wondered where his genes would go. Now I know for sure. You got them.'

Laura kept the smile on her face but she knew there was nothing of the dreamer in her. She was efficient, business-like, a planner not a dreamer and she was aiming to be more efficient in the future. She had the responsibility of Tony. She was completely accustomed to her life revolving around him. He anchored her to the ground and would do for a good many years.

In the small, dark office of Albright and Durban, Mr Albright searched his desk, a surprised look on his face as if he'd never had an appointment with them at all.

'Your father's will, yes. He sent it before he died and then he came back and died right here in England.'

He tutted away and Laura watched him, trying not to show her impatience. Albright didn't seem to be a good name for a man who was dour and dry as the dust that covered his tomes of legal publications. He'd been her mother's solicitor too, for a very brief time. They'd never had enough money to need a family solicitor.

'Mmm, yes, I have it here.' He opened a long envelope after searching the cluttered top of his desk. 'In a nutshell, your father, Charles Hughes, left everything equally to both of you. He seems to have known your mother was already dead. Though how he knew that…' Albright pulled himself out of this speculative mood and read on. 'There is property in Canada—a ranch called Blue Moon. There's also a sealed letter addressed to you.'

He frowned over the top of his spectacles at Laura and she understood by his expression that the letter should not have been sealed and that the ranch had an inappropriate name.

It wasn't inappropriate to her and she nearly laughed aloud.

Blue Moon. It reminded her of everything her father had been because it was a favourite saying of her mother. 'We'll never see him in a blue moon.' It had been said with bitterness, probably said to her father plenty of times too.

So he'd done it. He'd finally found his Eldorado. For the first time she wondered if he'd been happy, if he'd had friends. Both she and Tony only knew one side of things—their mother's side.

Laura looked across at her brother and he was spell-bound, staring at Albright as if the man had pulled a big white rabbit out of the envelope instead of a will.

'A ranch?' Tony sounded unbelieving. He sounded rather like a young boy, the boy he'd never really had the chance to be.

Laura almost held her breath in case she'd misheard.

'I know nothing further,' Albright said with a reproving glance when they both continued to stare at him. 'It's more of a letter than a real will but it's legal enough, signed by witnesses and sent from a solicitor in Alberta. Anything further you need to know you can find out from there.'

Laura stretched out her hand when he simply stood, as if he was thinking of lecturing them. 'We'll enquire. I assume the address is on the document?'

'As I said, it's more of a letter than a will. I'm not sure if it could be called a document. Everything has been done from Edmonton.'

'Then we'll see to it.' Laura stood and quickly took the envelope. She didn't like being here. She hadn't liked coming here when her mother had died. Mr Albright had spoken to them then as if they were both small children and he seemed to feel the need to lecture them on this occasion too.

'I wanted to see you in any case,' he said sharply, before she could make it to the door. 'There's the matter of the house you're living in at the moment. As you know, your mother only rented it and I happen to know the owner. He was worried about getting in touch with you when you were recently bereaved but he's anxious to sell the place. I took the liberty of telling him that you were in no position to buy.'

Laura was instantly on the offensive, her wide, dark eyes narrowed as she turned back to face him. 'And he's in no position to throw us out,' she snapped. 'We're tenants.'

'Well, no, you're not legally tenants. Your mother was the tenant. He can certainly ask you to leave. In point of fact he could have asked you to leave six months ago. He's been kind enough to let things go on as they were so far but house prices are beginning to fall. He wants to sell as soon as possible.'

'He'll have a hard time doing that,' Laura retorted, glaring at Albright now. 'The rent is paid regularly. The place is in good order and I took over the tenancy when mother died.'

'I understand you have nothing written down. Nothing that legally binds the tenancy to you?'

Laura's dark eyes blazed. 'Just whose solicitor are you, Mr Albright? You were supposed to represent my mother and, it seems, my father. Now you're intervening on behalf of the owner of the property we live in. Isn't that a conflict of interests?'

His sallow face flushed bright red. 'My responsibility to your mother died with her and as to your father, he seemed to think he could use this firm simply as a post office for the will and letter. He could equally have written directly to you.'

No, her father could not have written to them. He would have been too ashamed at the way he'd deserted them so long ago. He hadn't known them now. She wondered if he'd ever written to her mother.

'If we move, it will be when we're good and ready,' she snapped, determined to fight for their rights. 'The owner couldn't throw us out without a lot of hassle and a court battle. He knows it. So do you, Mr Albright.'

Tony suddenly chipped in. 'We've got a ranch in Canada now, haven't we?'

'We have and that's where we'll go—when we get around to it.'

Laura hustled Tony outside before Mr Albright could compose another legal sermon. She was shaking with annoyance but when she looked at Tony he was grinning.

'That put him in his place,' he said with a satisfied nod. 'Bet Albright never expected you to go for his throat. Silly old devil. He's just like everybody else in this poky little town, full of his own importance. Doesn't matter to us now, though. We're getting out. We're going to the wide open spaces. We're ranchers!'

He grabbed Laura and spun her round in the street and, though she felt a little embarrassed by the looks they drew, she couldn't help the light-hearted feeling that came when she realised Tony was acting like an excited boy.

'Not so fast,' Laura gasped when she had her breath back. 'We don't know a thing about this. It might all be a pipedream. Dad was like that.'

'You heard what that old coot said, "it's legal enough, signed by witnesses and sent from a solicitor in Alberta".' Tony gave a wickedly accurate imitation of Albright's voice. 'It can't be a pipedream, Laurie. It's got to be a real place or a solicitor wouldn't have signed it.'

Laura shook her fair head. 'I suppose you're right. All the same…'

When they came to her car Tony took the wheel himself. He'd passed his test with the same capability he did everything else. He'd always been ahead of his age in school and now he had a university place at seventeen. Laura was proud of him but she knew he'd never had any fun, never done the things teenagers did.

Neither had she for that matter. She was twenty-five and a very efficient personal assistant to the managing director of a local industrial firm but she'd never really enjoyed herself. Both she and Tony had been weighed down with responsibilities while their mother had gone out to work.

She realised too that they had both felt guilty about it. They had listened since they were far too young to the grumbles of a woman who had been deserted.

Why hadn't their mother divorced Charles Hughes? It sometimes seemed to Laura that her mother had simply enjoyed the martyrdom. When the thought sneaked into her brain, Laura felt the old rush of guilt.

Tony glanced at her. 'You're trying to find snags, Laurie. You're doing that thinking again. Please don't. For the first time in either of our lives we have the chance to fly free. You've never had the chance. You took your exams and went straight into a job, although you were clever enough to go to university. Mother wouldn't have liked that. She wouldn't have had anyone to gripe at. And I know you did it for me so that I wouldn't be at the receiving end of all her grumbles. I know you've been saving up for me to go to university with plenty of money when you should have been buying clothes and make-up, having holidays. You've never even had a man calling around until Bruce.'

Laura couldn't argue. He was right about everything. She thought she'd been protecting him but he'd noticed all the same. Bruce could be called a long-term suitor, definitely her mother's choice. He was always *there* whether she liked it or not. He had spent hours talking to her mother. His whole attitude made Laura feel like a Victorian spinster.

She gave a heartfelt sigh. 'Going off to Canada might be a wild-goose chase. Dad was unreliable.'

'This is not one of his dreams that Mum used to talk about. This is real, legal, definite. There's a ranch in Canada and it's ours. For once in our lives let's do something extravagant and risky. It might be the only chance we ever get.'

Laura bit at her lip. 'That sounds depressing.'

'I've felt depressed plenty of times when I saw you cheerfully going off to work. You should have been enjoying university. I've felt depressed when I've heard Mother telling you how hard life was. I know you tend to laugh things off but she had us both trapped, didn't she? There was no need for her to stick grimly to the past. She could have married again, been happy, allowed us to be happy. Fly free, Laurie. Please. Just this once.'

They sat in the car when they came to the house and Laura looked up at it and saw the semi-detached house they had always lived in. They had good, quiet neighbours, which was fortunate, but even from the car the house looked dreary.

This was their chance to get away. Dared she take it? Dared she take the responsibility for the gamble? She knew it was a gamble but Tony was right. There might never be another chance.

'I'll write to the solicitor in Alberta and see what he says.'

'Don't write. Let's just go,' Tony urged enthusiastically.

Laura followed him indoors, her stomach churning with anxiety. She spent her time worrying about Tony's lack of youthful enjoyment yet wasn't she the same? Everything he'd said was true and she knew it.

She'd reached twenty-five and yet she'd never had a serious love affair, never gone off on her own, not even to university. She was clever and yet she crushed it. She had crushed every soaring hope, every dream and had placed responsibility in their place.

Even Bruce Martin was someone her mother had encouraged her to see. He held her hand, kissed her lightly, took her to the cinema, took her for a drink and a meal, brought her home and said goodbye like a brother.

Nothing in her life was exciting, never had been exciting. All dreams had been carefully hidden and squashed. She worried about Tony and she should also have been worried about herself. At this rate she was going to follow in her mother's footsteps. Goodness, she'd been well trained. The thought of Bruce hanging around for the rest of her life was horrifying. She was free now, wasn't she?

Laura put her bag down on the table and turned to Tony, who was watching her with his usual anxiety. She carefully drew the letter out of the envelope, realising that she didn't even know her father's handwriting. She took a big breath, began to read and soon became absorbed. The letter was filled with the joy of life, a joy that neither she nor Tony had ever been able to feel.

Dear Laura,

I'm writing to you and not your brother because you may just remember me. I remember you and, believe it or not, I still miss you. Many times I've thought of coming to get you but I still think of you as my little girl and you'll be a grown woman now.

I moved up to Canada years ago and as I grow older I've a great desire in me for you to see this place. I live on a ranch in the shadow of the Rocky Mountains. It's so beautiful here that every morning I stand and stare for a long time before I start out on my horse for the day.

You would love the horses and love watching the cattle roam over the prairie. You would love listening to the sound of the wind and seeing the great, wide skies. There's freedom here, Laura.

I've got a great friend called Josh. We go on fishing trips into the mountains and you should see the lakes up there. They're bluer than the sky and filled with rainbow trout. There's the wonderful ranch set in the foothills and it's home to me.

When I die I'm leaving everything to my two children. I know what it's like in England and there must be something of me in you. This is a good life. Make use of it, enjoy it like I've done. I really want you to come here and take up where I leave off. I know I shouldn't have left you but I had to follow my dream. Follow the same dream and you won't regret it.

The letter was just signed, 'Your Father.'

Tony was watching and as Laura handed the letter to him she realised that her excuses for not going to Canada were now ended. There was the letter and there was the will. It was all real and she couldn't believe the good fortune that would turn their lives around.

She wanted to go, she wanted to make her father's dream come true if nothing else. Tears came into her eyes. There was a loneliness in the letter that perhaps he hadn't even known himself.

When Tony finished reading, Laura looked across at him.

'It's true, isn't it?'

'Well, I can't see anything wrong with it. I know how your mind works, Laurie, but even if we'll be taking a chance, we're going to something that's definite.'

'Have you noticed the date on his letter? He wrote it three years ago and never sent it.'

'I noticed. You know what I think? He was too nervous to write to us. We've no real idea of what went on between him and Mum. We really don't know whether he wrote to her, do we? If he did, she probably told him we were better off without him. The more I think about it, the more excuses I can find for him.'

The same thoughts had been running through Laura's mind. If her mother had said that then he would have felt there was nothing to come back to.

She picked up the phone and dialled the number at the top of the letter from her father's solicitor in Edmonton, Alberta. Her mind was made up. It might be taking a chance but it was the only chance they were likely to get and they owed it to their father to go to Canada and at least to look at his home.

*   *   *

When Bruce came, Laura caught Tony before she answered the door. 'Stick around, please. I don't want to face this by myself. I know he'll disapprove and then I'll lose my temper.'

'Oh, I wouldn't miss it for the world, especially the temper bit,' Tony said, grinning widely. 'In fact, I'll answer the door. Make him a cup of tea, he's going to need it.'

Bruce had thick, sandy hair and, although he was good-looking enough, he had the same sort of expression on his face that Mr Albright had. He certainly disapproved. Laura realised he disapproved of plenty of things as a matter of course. She also realised she was being channelled into the sort of life her mother had laid out for her and that Bruce endorsed. Without the letter from her father she would have walked right into the trap. If her father had had nothing else to leave to her, at least he had left that—the power to see what her life would become here.

'It's a hare-brained idea,' Bruce snapped when they explained their plans. 'Your mother used to tell me about the sort of person your father was. You're proposing to go out to Canada with the same happy-go-lucky thoughts he had.'

'You never knew him,' Laura said sharply.

'Neither did you,' he countered. 'What you *did* know about him should have made you wary. I heard plenty from your mother. Even though he's dead, you'll be putting yourself at his mercy, just like your mother did.'

'If we stay on here we'll be as dismal as the people round here,' Tony intervened. He was about to say, As dismal as you are, but he caught Laura's quick frown of warning and left it at that.

'We've got nothing to lose,' Laura said firmly. 'According to Mr Albright we're about to be evicted from this house so we'll have to move in any case.'

'You can take the landlord to court.' Bruce was about to

get on his high horse about it but Tony stepped in at that point.

'We'd rather take what money we've got and risk it on going to Canada.'

'What money Laura's got, you mean.'

Bruce looked angry and Tony went red with annoyance. Laura stopped that line of talk at once.

'Tony and I share everything, including decisions.' She was frowning and really sharp now. 'We've decided to take the risk of going to Canada. I've already phoned Edmonton and they told us to go on to a place called Leviston and find the ranch from there. We're going, Bruce, so save your breath. For once in our lives we're doing exactly as we like.'

Bruce got up and began to pace about. He was obviously furious—more furious, Laura thought, because nobody had asked his opinion.

'I can foresee the time when you'll be stuck out there in the Great Emptiness with no money left,' he said, swinging round to glare at them both. 'Have you any plans for such a predicament?'

'I'll work. I've never done anything else but work, so it will be no surprise.'

'For God's sake, Laura! This is so much pie in the sky. You should have talked it over with me.'

'It's our pie and our sky,' Laura flared. 'I didn't need to talk it over. I'm quite capable of making up my own mind.'

Bruce started for the door. He was too irritated by Laura's stubbornness to stay longer. His domineering attitude hadn't worked. 'I'll call tomorrow, Laura. You're really too practical to do something like this. A good night's sleep will bring you to your senses.'

'Will it?' Tony looked at her worriedly when the door slammed behind Bruce.

'I've already come to my senses. We leave for Canada as soon as we can and if it turns out to be pie in the sky, well, as I said, it's our pie and our sky. If nothing else we'll have travelled and maybe we'll have to come back, but not to this town and not to that Bruce.'

Just over a month later, Laura and Tony stood in the small and only hotel Leviston possessed. Tony was still excited but Laura was a bit worried and a lot tired. For someone who had never travelled before, she had found the journey to Canada and then across to Leviston exhausting.

In Edmonton there had been no further information for her. A harassed-looking man had told her that their father had simply walked in off the street and asked them to draw up a will. Any further details were at the small town of Leviston.

Well, they were here. It was late afternoon and they had arrived by train only a few minutes ago. Leviston was set in the foothills of the towering Rocky Mountains and, although it was certainly a small town, the presence of the great mountain range made it seem smaller still.

The mountains seemed to dominate everything and Laura wasn't at all accustomed to the silence that seemed to hover over the town.

All the way here on the train she had stared from the window at the huge landscape and Bruce's words had rung round in her head—the Great Emptiness. It really seemed to be that and, after living all her life in England's cosy atmosphere, she felt overwhelmed by the size of things.

There had just seemed to be great stretches of empty landscape, rocky outcrops and deep pine forests. Occasionally she had seen cattle roaming across grassland. Once, she saw a deer standing, watching the train go by.

But she was used to towns, to people, and she wondered

where they would get help if they needed it. There seemed to be nothing but this wide, silent landscape. Where would she find this mythological job if things went wrong?

Now, with their luggage on the floor beside them, Laura was in conversation with the kindly looking owner of the small hotel. There was no doubt that they would have to stay for the night and Laura's mind was doing a quick calculation of what the cost would be. Already they had spent much more than she'd expected and Tony looked younger than ever.

'Blue Moon Ranch? Can't say I've ever heard of it.' Al Bisley scratched the shock of brown hair that was combed closely to his head. 'I've lived here most of my life but that name just doesn't ring any sort of bell.'

'But it must be here,' Laura persisted. 'We called at my father's solicitors in Edmonton and we were told to come here. In any case, my father wrote to us and his letter is headed Blue Moon, Leviston. According to the firm in Edmonton, his friend Josh will show us everything and help us.'

He looked at her sharply. 'What did you say your name was?'

'I'm Laura Hughes. This is my brother Tony.'

Al Bisley's face seemed to freeze over before it took on a very wary expression.

'Hughes? Then you must be Charlie's girl. I don't know what name he gave his place. Didn't even know it had a name. I've never seen it myself but it's on the edge of the Wexford ranch.'

'Next to it?'

'Er—you could say that,' he muttered. 'The Bar W was Josh Wexford's place. It's been in the Wexford family for as long back as anyone can remember.'

Al Bisley was getting more agitated by the minute and

he looked up in obvious relief when a red Ford Explorer pulled in at the front of the hotel. The frozen expression left his face but not the anxiety.

'Here's Cal Wexford now. He'll know what to do.'

The way he said it made Laura think that Cal Wexford was the sort of person who always knew what to do. She hoped so. She was almost too tired to stand and she was worried about plenty of things.

All their furniture was in store back in England and that had been expensive. She had insisted on getting return tickets when they'd booked their flight but there had been such a long way to come after that. They had been forced to stay in Edmonton for a day and then take the train here. They couldn't just hang around and enjoy themselves. They couldn't afford a holiday and she was beginning to realise just how little money they had.

They were all standing in silence, looking at the door and unmistakably waiting like a small committee, when a tall frame filled the doorway.

The newcomer looked completely taken aback at the rapt attention he was getting. Black eyebrows shot up in astonishment and then he grinned. It was a pleasant, agreeable grin that lit up a handsome, very masculine face and showed white, even teeth.

Laura felt something she'd never felt before, a rush of sensation that made her face flush. She felt as if she was sparkling all over with an awareness she couldn't quite cope with.

Cal Wexford was tall, lean and powerful-looking. He was about six one or two and seemed to tower over them all, even from the doorway. When he stepped forward from the shadow of the entrance she could see he had black hair that gleamed with health and blue eyes sparkling with amusement.

He was the most strikingly handsome man she'd ever seen. In jeans and a denim jacket that fitted across broad shoulders he looked at ease with the world and more sure of himself than any man Laura had ever met.

'You got a problem, Al, or is this some sort of new initiation ceremony you've been working on?'

He was still smiling as he came forward and Al Bisley spoke in a hurry, anxious to get the words out before Cal Wexford came any closer.

'*I* don't have a problem, Cal. I expect you'll sort this all out as you'll be involved. This is Laura Hughes and her brother. They came from England to see Blue Moon. They've come from Charlie's solicitor in Edmonton.'

The smile died on Wexford's face as he heard the quick rush of words. He came to an abrupt halt and said something under his breath that sounded very much like 'God Almighty' to Laura.

His face took on an altogether different look and he didn't seem warm and friendly any more. He looked hard and immovable as granite. His eyes were now so brilliantly blue that they seemed to scorch the air.

He stared at Laura, ignoring Tony, and she felt too jaded to face him right then. If he said anything nasty she knew she was going to sit down on the suitcases and just howl. Every bit of tiredness she had felt before she saw him came sweeping back in a rush. She certainly didn't feel upbeat about anything. Facing that look, she felt about as determined as a frightened rabbit.

Wexford looked her over in that stare, noting her slender figure in her tan trouser suit, her astonishing silver-blonde hair that reached beyond her shoulders and the dark eyes ringed with tiredness. He seemed to be staring at her intently for a long time and nobody had the nerve to speak at all.

The blue eyes seemed to see right through Laura until she felt uncomfortably vulnerable.

He turned his attention on Tony then, and saw Charlie's looks staring right back at him. There was the same light brown hair, almost fair but not quite. There were the same tawny eyes and good-looking face. These two were Charlie's children all right. Damn it, he would have strangled the man if he'd been here right now.

'Where's your father?' He snapped out the question at Laura, his attention now riveted on her again, and she faded right before his eyes. The sweetly beautiful face became even more pale and she sank down onto a suitcase, looking as if her legs wouldn't hold her up any more.

'My father died just over a month ago, Mr Wexford. He came back to England to die. Our solicitor gave us a letter from him and a will. My—my father left us the Blue Moon and now we're trying to find it. He said his friend Josh would show us the place.'

At the sound of her voice he felt a long tug of feeling inside that set his blood racing. She was beautiful. She looked like a startled fawn with those great big brown eyes and her slender appearance. She also looked like an angel with that silver-blonde hair, but looked ready to run or fight her way out of here.

He didn't say anything for a moment. He just went on giving her that penetrating look and it was impossible to tell anything from his expression. But the brain behind the handsome face was working fast and Laura was aware of that as she sat watching him in anxious silence.

Behind her, she heard Al Bisley give an uncomfortable little cough and the blue eyes released her from the pressure, like a light being switched off. He just seemed to power down and become normal and Laura took a shaky breath as her heart stopped thundering like a mad thing.

'Well, now you've almost found the place, Miss Hughes. It's right next to the Bar W. Let's get you out there before nightfall.'

She stared at him, her eyes looking too big for her face. 'But—but you don't know us at all.'

One dark brow rose sceptically. 'I knew Charlie. I knew him very well indeed. You want to know where Blue Moon is. I'm about to show you.'

CHAPTER TWO

CAL strode forward and helped her to her feet and even through her tiredness Laura could feel the sparks that seemed to fly from his fingers. She could also feel the heat that came into her face when he shot her a quick, burning glance.

It was something she'd never felt before and she didn't know what it was. It felt like excitement—or fear. It could easily have been fear because all her determination had suddenly gone and she found herself feeling lost, unable to help her brother at all.

Wexford lifted the luggage as if it were made of paper and nodded to Tony to bring the rest.

'I'm real sorry to drop this on you, Cal,' Al muttered.

'I'll deal with it,' Wexford said with enough abruptness for Laura to feel the need to intervene.

'You don't have to deal with us, Mr Wexford,' she protested, fighting off her tiredness. 'We're more than capable of seeing to ourselves. We'll stay here tonight and then search further in the morning.'

He looked her up and down. It wasn't an insolent look but the searing blue eyes took in far more than she was prepared to show.

'Oh, you will, will you?' He glanced across at Al Bisley. 'I guess you don't have any spare rooms for the night, Al?'

'Er—no, as a matter of fact we're full up.'

Laura looked round at him helplessly. She knew he was lying. She also knew this was the only hotel and that she was dropping where she stood. All the same, she wasn't

24

about to be dragged forth by this man and taken to some place she hadn't even seen. In spite of the emotional effect he had on her, she was too streetwise for that.

She drew in a deep breath and stood her ground firmly. 'All the same, we'll manage, thank you, Mr Wexford.'

Cal Wexford looked exasperated. He had two suitcases swinging from his brown hands and another one under his arm. For one scary moment he looked as if he was contemplating putting her under the other arm, and then his face relaxed.

'Look,' he said quietly. 'It's not your fault that Charlie Hughes was your father and I'll admit that if he was here at the present time he'd feel the sharp edge of my tongue. Even so, Charlie was a friend of my father, his best friend. They did things together for years but Josh can't help you now because he's dead too. When you start looking for Blue Moon you're going to have to cross my property. You may as well start putting up with me now because I'm unavoidable. I'll take on my father's promise to Charlie.' He turned to Tony. 'Come on, Tiger. You wanted to see a ranch. You're about to see one.'

'You mean you're taking us to *your* ranch?' Tony asked, speaking for the first time as they went out through the open door.

'That's what it looks like,' Cal muttered. 'Drop the cases in the Ford and let's move. Your sister looks as if she needs a good hot meal and a warm, soft bed. She'll get both at the Bar W.'

'But we can't just ask you to...' Laura began, but he ignored her and held the door open for her when he'd put the luggage into the back.

'Did you ask? I never heard that, Miss Hughes. People don't need to ask around here. We're hospitable.'

Laura climbed into the front seat and sat clutching her

bag. She was too tired to think and, in any case, there was something about Cal Wexford that excluded thinking. He seemed to be as inevitable as the coming night.

Al Bisley called from the doorway. 'Hey, Cal. Did you want something? I guess you must have or you wouldn't have called in.'

The brilliantly blue eyes shot him an ironic look. 'Oh, I certainly wanted something, but right now I can't remember what it was. I'll send one of the boys down if it comes to mind.'

Laura knew what had made him forget—if he had. It was his determination to contend with two people he'd never seen before in his life. Her father's friend Josh was dead and his son was about to put up with them for that reason.

She looked up and saw the Rocky Mountains in the distance. The sun was going down behind them, making the heights stand out black and stark against a sky that was flooded with glorious colour. There was the glitter of snow and ice on the peaks that caught the setting sun in a shower of sparkling white.

It looked beautiful, lonely, remote and forbidding. Somehow it reminded her of all the responsibilities she carried, responsibilities that seemed too big to contend with at the moment.

This man was offering charity as far as she could tell and her mind would normally have recoiled at the idea, but right now Laura was too tired and worn to even worry about that. She simply closed her eyes and shut everything out.

Before they even reached the edge of town, Laura was deeply asleep, and after a while her head fell to Cal's shoulder. He ignored it and ignored the quick pull of awareness that shot through him. He drove on but when she snuggled herself into a more comfortable position he had to move to accommodate her. His dark brows rose in amused surprise and he shot a quick glance at her fair head.

From the back seat, Tony was watching through the mirror and Cal met his eyes.

'Laura's very tired,' Tony explained. 'She's hardly slept since we left England. She feels responsible for me, although I'm capable of taking care of myself. She always feels responsible for everything. I can move her, if you like.'

'Leave her. She seems comfortable enough. We'll wake her when we get home.'

Cal was aware that Tony was still watching him intently and he decided this was a good chance to get to know something without the beautiful sister staring at him like a determined doe and chipping in with explanations of how they could manage by themselves.

He already suspected that they couldn't. They had simply come here without any preparation, as far as he could see. He was also trying to get used to the surge of feeling that had raced through his body at the sight of Laura. It was something that needed thinking about and he knew that, Charlie or not, he would have hung around town if she'd been staying there.

He liked having her head on his shoulder. For one wild moment he wished she were even closer.

'Tell me what started you off on this jaunt to the Rockies? Were you planning to sell Charlie's place and then go back to England?' He glanced in the mirror as he spoke and was in time to see disappointment on Tony's face.

'I think Laura has a plan like that, but I was hoping to settle here. I thought I might be able to persuade her to stay. We didn't know Dad. He left when Laura was eight and she's twenty-five now. I've never even seen him because Mother didn't keep any pictures of him in the house.'

'Not surprising, is it? Seventeen years is a long time.'

'Mum could have married again. Laura took the brunt of all the gripes, she cheerfully gave up everything for me. She's given up everything again—although I'm glad she gave up Bland Bruce.'

Cal was surprised into a grin. 'I take it that was the boyfriend?'

Tony hitched forward and lowered his voice. 'In a way, although I'm not sure what way. You couldn't really say he was a boyfriend. Let's just say that Mother approved. Bruce tried to persuade us not to come but Laura can be really tough when she sets her mind to it. Nobody can bully Laura.'

Cal glanced down at her again. She didn't look tough to him, but it seemed she was the mainstay of her brother's life. She only looked like a teenager herself. He wouldn't have guessed she was twenty-five. Still, being thirty-four himself and used to running a big ranch from boyhood, he imagined he seemed like a dictatorial adult to these two babes in the wood.

'So Bruce didn't like the idea of you coming to Canada?'

Tony pulled a disgusted face. 'He said it was pie in the sky but Laura really snapped at him then, so he went home. By the time he came again we'd got everything worked out. Somehow or other, though, I hoped to be able to just come to Blue Moon and take over bit by bit. I expect it was just a dream, though. Laura never has stupid dreams. She's down-to-earth.'

Cal decided to keep quiet about Blue Moon. Time enough for them to find out when they were rested. It was too late to make any sort of move today in any case. Night was coming and a storm by the look of the sky. He had to get these two weary travellers settled at the ranch and then he had to do some thinking. He had to think how he could keep Laura close while he decided what it was that was sticking hot knives into his insides.

'Taking over a ranch is easier said than done, Tiger. To-night you'll stay at the Bar W and tomorrow we'll think things over.'

'What things?' Tony looked hopeful and Cal sighed.

'Damned if I know,' he muttered to himself. Truth to tell, he was dreading having to explain to both of them, but most of all he wanted to see a smile on Laura's pale face.

He knew he had about as much chance of that as he had of lifting a horse off the ground. She looked completely worn out. So she had no dreams. That was another black mark against Charlie.

Laura stayed asleep until they actually drew up outside the ranch house. She woke up when Cal gently moved her head from his shoulder and she was instantly embarrassed and flustered.

'I fell asleep. I'm so sorry.'

'You were tired. What's to be sorry about? Tony and I had a nice long conversation while you slept. We've decided that, with night coming on, it's better to leave things until morning.' He came to help her out and simply gripped her waist and lifted her down when she started to move. 'Leave the cases. One of the boys will bring those up. Meanwhile let's get you inside before the storm breaks.'

'I'll bring them, Mr Wexford,' Tony offered.

'Okay. We'll do it together in a minute and give the boys a break. Let's get into the house, though. By the way, my name is Cal. You'd better call me that, Tiger.'

Tony grinned widely. 'My name is Tony.'

'Too late. I've christened you Tiger. That's what you'll get from now on. I'm not one to change my mind.'

Laura stood listening to this humorous exchange, startled that the two had got to this stage of acquaintance while she'd slept. She seemed to have gone to sleep scared and wakened to find they had acquired a determined guardian. She was still tingling from the unexpected touch of his hands on her waist as he'd lifted her from the car.

'Mr Wexford…' she began, but he took her arm in a no-nonsense grip and turned her to the ranch house.

'It's Cal and you'll notice I'm considerably bigger than you. If you want to argue we'll do it in the morning. Even then, I'll still be bigger than you and, as I've got your luggage, I guess the cards are stacked against you, Miss Hughes.'

'Please…please call me Laura.' She glanced at him anxiously. 'I don't know why you're being so nice to us. I realise that you never expected to see us and I know something's wrong. There's no Blue Moon, is there?'

Cal's face took on its stony expression again and he didn't look at her.

'Oh, there's a Blue Moon, all right. You'll see it tomorrow. As I said, it's going to be too dark to get over there tonight so you'll stay here.'

'But why? We're nothing to you. You've never seen us before.'

'Did I forget to mention that I'm a saint? But don't go calling me Saint Cal. The boys might try to take advantage and I'm not always feeling kindly disposed.'

He suddenly grinned when she looked up at him wildly. 'Relax. You made it to Canada in one piece and I'm not about to see you in trouble.'

'But you don't have to look after us like this.'

'Aw, drat! Just when I thought I'd found a nice new

hobby. Now I'll have to think of something else. Seems you've got a mean streak, ma'am.'

Laura shook her head and sighed loudly. 'I just don't understand you.'

Cal didn't answer but he was thinking that right now he didn't even understand himself, except that he wanted to keep her close until he found out just what was eating at him.

What he *did* know was that tomorrow he had to break the news to them and they'd come a long way to be disappointed.

He knew his father would have found the whole thing eye-poppingly amusing. He wasn't like his father. He didn't find anything about it amusing and he hadn't needed to see any legal document either. It was all true. As soon as he'd seen them standing in Al Bisley's hotel he'd known it was true.

Laura Hughes was a slender picture, a beautiful princess lost in the woods. She came just higher than his shoulder and he couldn't imagine her being able to snap at anyone. But Tony looked like Charlie—the old so and so. He'd deserted them all those years ago and then left them with this predicament. If Josh Wexford and Charlie Hughes had still been here he would have banged their heads together with a God Almighty crash.

'Oh, it's so lovely!' Laura's soft exclamation brought Cal back out of his irate fantasy of violence. She was looking up at the ranch house and the foothills far behind it that were the vanguard to the high Rocky Mountains.

Cal stopped beside her, suddenly seeing his home through her eyes. Set on higher ground, the house was a sprawling two-storeyed ranch house, stone-built and impervious to any weather the Rockies could throw at it. Behind it was more rising ground, liberally covered with pine, aspen and white birch. The Rocky Mountains in the far distance made a grand backdrop and the sun, still sinking behind the snow-covered peaks, was sparkling off glaciers that never melted.

'Yes. It's beautiful if you can take the life,' he agreed. 'It's hot in summer and damned cold in winter. The cattle roam all over and plenty get lost in the high woods. They're ornery and stupid. The men have to fetch them down before they either go wild or die.'

'Don't you like it?' Laura looked up·at him and the severe expression on his face softened as he looked towards the hills.

'I wouldn't want to be anywhere else in the whole world. When I have to go away, I can't wait to get back. I was born here and I'll die here. I've run this place since I was about eighteen. Sometimes I feel as if I'm as planted here as the Rockies.'

Laura watched him for a moment and then turned to the ranch house where lights were coming on because of the gathering storm.

'That's wonderful.' She sighed. 'To really belong, to know who you are. It explains your hospitality.'

Cal was a little baffled as to how she'd reached this conclusion, but he didn't have time to try and sort it out. He supposed it was difficult to know where you belonged when you had a father like Charlie.

Tony was hanging back, looking around, and he wanted to know where the men slept.

'In their quarters.' Cal's hand made a wide sweep of the garden and showed him where the ranch buildings began. 'We used to have a bunk house and they all settled together. Now they get private accommodation. The other buildings are barns, stables and grain stores. I'll show you in the morning. Right now we'd better get inside because when the rain comes it's likely to be heavy.'

'Tomorrow we'll be seeing Blue Moon?' Tony asked eagerly and Cal nodded, back to his tight-faced expression.

'Sure,' he said, and Tony cast an anxious glance towards Laura. Her moment of magic when she'd seen the ranch faded as swiftly as it had come. Something was wrong and Cal Wexford didn't want to tell them.

Inside the ranch house she was mesmerised all over again. For the first time in her life she was standing in a huge house. The floor was pine, polished to a brilliance that shone in the lights, and the hall was wide as a dance hall. It was long and had a meandering look about it that said the house had been built in one design and then added to when the need had arisen. Doors led from the hall and a great curved staircase, too grand to be true, stretched to the upper floor.

Laura was enchanted. She'd never expected to see such a glamorous place out in the wilds of Canada. Tony was fascinated too.

'It's like Dallas,' he said in an awestricken voice. 'What do you call it?'

'We call it the Bar W.' Cal laughed, setting the luggage down. 'Believe it or not, this place started as a one-storeyed cabin. My great-grandfather drove a herd of cattle up here from Montana and built a cabin on this spot. When he was settled, my great-grandmother joined him and she wasn't a bit impressed. So pieces were added. They've been slowly added since then but I guess the improvements have finished now.'

'Oh, yes,' Laura breathed. 'It's perfect.' She flushed when he grinned down at her.

'You hear that Biddy?' he called as a slim, middle-aged woman came out from what was obviously the kitchen.

'She says my nest is perfect. That deserves a reward. What's for dinner?'

They were introduced as if they were honoured guests instead of absolute strangers of the nuisance variety who had just popped up from nowhere. Biddy Alders was the wife of the ranch foreman. She had frizzy hair that was an unlikely shade of red, but she was welcoming and businesslike.

'I'll see to your rooms, then I'll get the dinner,' she said. 'It's all ready so you'd better not be too long upstairs.'

'Biddy sees to the house and Frank sees to the ranch,' Cal explained seriously. 'Between them I get bossed around from morning to night.'

'Like to see anyone boss you around,' Biddy snorted. 'Everybody jumps when he cracks the whip,' she said in an aside to Laura. 'You've only seen his good side.'

Laura went up the stairs behind Biddy feeling dazed with everything. They had just been welcomed here with no questions asked. She was even more dazed when she saw her room. So far the house had breathed money at her and the room she went into was no exception. The colours were softly welcoming, the carpets were deep and she had her own bathroom.

Cal Wexford had grown up with this. No wonder he never wanted to move away. She thought of the dreary semi-detached house they'd left behind in England. Even that was not theirs any more.

If Blue Moon was non-existent then they were homeless, with little money and few prospects. She still had her job but that would never be enough to get a house and cover Tony's extra expenses at university. Laura felt almost panic-stricken at the thought of what would face her in England.

Later, after their luggage had been delivered to their

rooms, Laura went downstairs. Cal and Tony were already waiting for dinner and, apart from looking freshly washed, neither of them had changed. Cal was still in jeans but he was wearing a blue checked shirt that made his eyes look startling in the lights and Laura was glad she hadn't rushed to find something to change into that wasn't creased.

Biddy came in at once with the meal and Laura sat in silence as Cal poured wine for the three of them. He was silent and seemed to be thinking deeply.

'Does Biddy live in?' Laura asked finally, feeling she had to make conversation.

'No. Frank and Biddy have a house on the ranch. Two of the other wives help her in the house but nobody lives in. My father didn't like anyone living in and neither do I. It's one of the few things we agreed about.'

'My father spoke about someone called Josh in his letter. I didn't know his second name was Wexford until the man at the hotel told us.'

Cal raised one black eyebrow. 'I can imagine. Charlie and Josh were thick as thieves. They rode together, gambled together and drank together, but mostly they fished. It suited me fine,' he added when Laura looked guilty. 'It kept Josh out of my hair. Without Charlie he would have interfered with everything.'

'Wasn't your father interested in ranching?' Laura asked, remembering that Cal had said he'd run the ranch since he was about eighteen.

'Not so you'd notice. He started out interested but after Mom died he always seemed to be at a loose end. He wasn't much interested in anything. I suppose Charlie filled a need; at least he kept Josh occupied and out of my way.'

Laura was silent as she tried to eat the wonderfully cooked meal. The butterflies in her stomach were getting in the way and making it almost impossible to eat. She felt it was her duty to make conversation but it was hard. In the first place she felt like an intruder. In the second place she knew that Cal Wexford had disapproved of her father, in spite of what he'd just said.

There was also the strange, exciting but uncomfortable feeling she had when Cal looked at her. His eyes were blue enough to drown in and he looked straight at her when she spoke. His gaze lingered, giving her more attention than she was used to, more than she could cope with.

She was dreading the morning too, because she knew they were going to find out something that would shatter them. It was kindness that kept Cal Wexford quiet about it, but she would rather have known now. She was used to disappointment, well able to stifle her feelings, but this time it was different. They had their furniture in store and she still had her job, but the money was almost gone. They had burned their boats in a big way. A sharp tongue wouldn't get her out of this predicament.

Tony started asking about the Bar W and Cal's attention turned to him as he answered. Laura was glad he wasn't looking at her any more. He was too disturbing and made her heart beat too fast. He had a way of holding her gaze until she felt fluttery inside. In any case, she wanted to calculate money and try to come up with a plan in case Blue Moon turned out to be hopeless. She was half asleep too.

She only came back to the present when Cal said, 'You'd better go and get into that warm bed before you fall on the floor.'

Laura was flustered, a guest who behaved inexcusably. Her dark eyes looked too big for her face again as she glanced up at him. 'I'm sorry,' she said quietly, but Cal stood up and helped her to her feet.

'Not as sorry as you would be if you fell to the floor,'

he remarked gently. 'Go to bed now and you'll feel fine in the morning.'

He didn't exactly look as if he believed what he was saying and she knew that morning would bring fresh problems.

Later, while she was getting ready for bed, Tony tapped on her door. He was standing in the passage when she answered and he was looking miserable.

'Laurie, I know you're tired but I just had to come and speak to you,' he said in a low voice. 'There's something wrong, isn't there? Mr Wexford is just being good to us. There's no Blue Moon Ranch and no land. What are we going to do?'

Cal was just going across the hall and he drew back under the high curve of the stairs when he heard Tony's words. He didn't want to eavesdrop but he didn't want to embarrass them by suddenly popping out either.

'There *is* a Blue Moon,' Laura answered. 'I asked him and he said there was. I'm sure he wouldn't lie, but I'm also sure something's wrong. Whatever it is, we'll find out tomorrow.'

'I'd rather know now,' Tony muttered.

'That's what I thought but I'm glad he kept quiet. I don't think I could face anything else tonight.'

'It's all my fault,' Tony said miserably. 'I persuaded you to come. Maybe you should have listened to Bruce instead of me.'

'No, thanks,' Laura whispered. 'Whatever happens we've had an adventure and, if it's the last adventure we get in our lives, it's something to remember. Don't worry. It's a good thing even if it's the only thing.'

When the door closed and he heard Tony going to his own room, Cal walked silently across the hall to his study. He closed the door as quietly as possible and then put the lamps on. Now he had to do his thinking because he knew what they would say when they saw Blue Moon.

He thought of Laura's worried face, her lovely eyes edged with tiredness. He thought of Tony's impossible dreams that didn't stand a chance of coming true. He sat at his desk and threw his head back. He had to come up with something to keep them here. Besides, Tony was a good kid and Laura made his blood hum in his veins. He wasn't nearly ready to let her go away.

'Charlie,' he muttered, 'you always were a crazy so and so, but this is your best trick yet. I'm damned if I'll let you get away with it. If you and Josh are still together, splitting your sides at this joke, then I'm warning you—don't count your chickens.'

In the morning, Laura looked out of her window and now she could see the true extent of the ranch buildings. There was a neat garden round the house itself and a short drive-way that led down to the huge yard of the ranch. After that the buildings began and stretched out for a long way. With the one-storeyed stone and wooden quarters of the ranch hands, the whole place looked like a small village.

Everything was already alive with activity and she imagined it had been so for a long time because there would be too much to do in a place as big as this. Nobody would be lying in bed and she'd better get a move on herself.

Laura was just turning away when a horse came thundering into the main yard going fast and furious. The rider was Cal Wexford and he dismounted while the horse was still running. He simply stepped out of the saddle and walked angrily towards two of the men as the horse dropped into a walk.

He was very obviously annoyed and this morning he didn't look like the easygoing man of the night before. He looked every inch the rancher. He had a white Stetson pulled down over his eyes and though he still wore jeans he was now wearing cowboy boots and a leather waistcoat of some sort over his shirt.

He was scowling and somebody was about to get the sharp edge of his tongue, an expression he'd used in town. Biddy said everyone jumped when he cracked the whip. He was about to crack it now as far as Laura could see.

The two ranch hands looked guilty and didn't answer back when he spoke to them in obvious anger. They just nodded dolefully and then went quickly on their way, mounting up and riding out. Laura assumed they had been told to do something and had not done it. She knew now if she hadn't known before that Cal Wexford wasn't always kind and amusing.

He pushed his hat back with one thumb and then stood with hands on his hips as he glared around. His body language still spoke of subdued rage and nobody came to enquire what had annoyed him. The few men who were around were suddenly intent on their work.

He turned as an older man rode into the yard and dismounted to speak to him, and after a minute Cal's shoulders relaxed. When he turned to come up to the house he looked more normal. His rage had obviously drained away.

He also looked up at Laura's window as he came closer and she didn't have time to step back out of sight. His face split into a grin when he saw her standing there watching him, and before she could move he swept off his hat and made her an exaggerated bow.

Laura felt embarrassment rush all over her. Not only had he caught her watching him, he had caught her standing at the window in her nightie. No wonder he was grinning and she understood why those eyes looked as if they could see a long way—they could!

She made a quick retreat into the shower and put on some speed. Today she would find out about Blue Moon and she hoped it wasn't the thought of it that had made Cal so bad-tempered with the men.

When she went downstairs in jeans and a red shirt, the other two were already eating breakfast. Cal pulled her chair out and served her from the sideboard.

'You've been up a long time,' Laura pointed out, desperate to make conversation because he was still looking as if he might give one of those grins. 'I would have thought you'd have eaten before now.'

'I eat at five when there's only me. I eat with the boys in the cookhouse. Now I've got guests so I'm eating with you.'

'You've been working since five?' Tony asked in astonishment.

'I always am, unless there's a holiday. There aren't many of those around here because the stock don't understand about holidays. We have to cover for anyone who's off, whether it's Christmas or not.' He looked seriously at Tony. 'Owning a ranch is a big responsibility, Tiger. But we get to take it easy sometimes, especially when there's thick snow and we can't take the horses out. Of course, then, we have to dig cattle out of the high drifts.'

Tony looked downcast and Cal was suddenly laughing.

'You're pulling my leg,' Tony accused.

'Honestly, I'm not. It's a great life out here—if you can take it. You still want to be a cowboy?'

'I'd jump at the chance,' Tony told him with a touch of defiance.

Cal nodded, watching him steadily, and then he said, with a quick change of subject, 'You mentioned last night that you were about to go to university.'

'I am, but I'm taking a year off first.'

'What are you going to do when you get to university?'

'Maths and computer studies, but I could still change my mind.'

Cal went on watching him and it looked to Laura as if he was summing things up. She didn't know what and she didn't know why but the butterflies started inside her again.

'What are you going to do with your year off, then?'

'I don't know. I'll have to get some sort of job to help out. I was going to get used to running a ranch but that's just a daydream, I suppose.'

'Dreams are what you make them,' Cal said, pushing his chair back. 'We'll get over to see Blue Moon if you're ready.' He shot Laura another glance of blue lightning. 'Don't suppose you can ride?'

'A horse, you mean? No, I can't. I've never had the chance.'

Cal gave a slight frown. No, he didn't suppose either of them had had the chance for much from what he'd gathered. Tony had been at school and his sister had been too busy working to take time off to enjoy herself. Too busy listening to their mother grumbling, according to Tony, too busy taking on the added burden of her young brother. And all the while, Charlie had been enjoying life.

'We'll take the Chevy. It's a pick-up though, and the going might be a bit rough.'

Laura jumped up and left the rest of her breakfast. 'Will we need coats? I—I noticed you had a leather waistcoat on when you rode into the yard?'

'That's part of the gear. In any case, I was going fast enough to make my own climate, but it's warm today. We often get nice weather in autumn. You'll not need a coat.'

He noticed her face was flushed and he managed not to grin. He knew what was bothering her—she was thinking about being at the window in her nightie. Remarking about how he'd looked when he came in had reminded her.

He would have liked to tell her that she looked stunning first thing in the morning, that she looked fit to eat in one big bite, but somehow he didn't think any remarks like that would go down well with Laura. She was too uptight. And she'd yet to see Blue Moon.

He glanced at Tony. 'Okay, Tiger, let's whistle and ride.'

Tony stuffed one last mouthful in and rushed to obey, although, by the look on his face, Laura thought he was also suffering from churning inside. She wasn't looking forward to this. Everything about Cal told her he wasn't looking forward to it either.

The pick-up had a bench seat in the front and they all sat together, Laura by Cal and Tony on the outside. There was a good deal of interest shown by the ranch hands who were still in the yard but, as far as Laura knew, nobody could guess why they were here.

One thing she had discovered, which wouldn't leave her mind: her father had been a drinker and a gambler. He had been well known around here but as to whether he had been well liked, apart from his friendship with Josh Wexford, she couldn't tell. She didn't think Cal had liked him, except for her father's obvious talent for keeping Josh Wexford occupied. She was beginning to wonder if her tears over the letter had been misplaced.

CHAPTER THREE

AFTER a few miles, they turned off the road and took a track south, with the foothills of the Rocky Mountains still close. Everything was beautiful and if Laura hadn't been filled with apprehension she would have enjoyed it much more.

There was the rolling prairie with cattle dotted here and there. There were clumps of smaller trees and then great stands of pine. She wanted to get out and walk, to drink in the serenity, to look and look because she felt that this would be the last time she would see the glorious sight.

They had always lived in a town and this was like paradise. She knew Tony was feeling the same because he was totally silent now.

They had to leave the track after a while and the Chevy pick-up bucked and reared over some pretty rough pastureland. Laura was thrown against Cal and she was embarrassed to find she liked that. She could smell the wonderful clean, tangy scent of his skin, she could feel the powerful muscles adjust as she was thrown against him. She loved seeing his capable brown hands on the wheel.

She almost jumped in shock when he glanced across and caught her watching him.

'I'm sorry about the rough ride,' he said, not taking his eyes from her. 'I can't do anything to catch you when you get jostled about. If I try to use one hand we'll end up in a gully.'

'It's all right,' Laura said quickly. 'I—I can see it's hard going to keep this pick-up straight.' She hoped he would think that was why she had been watching him, and she was careful not to do it again because his eyes seemed to see far too much and they made her pulse rate quicken.

A little while later he stopped beside a grove of aspen and invited them to get out. 'I'd like you to walk from here because I've got something to tell you.'

'You're going to tell us there's no Blue Moon,' Tony pronounced, looking as if he would take whatever blow was about to befall them.

'I'm not going to tell you that at all,' Cal said seriously. 'If there'd been no Blue Moon I would have told you back in Leviston. Blue Moon is just over the ridge. Before you see it I'll have to explain, though. It's got a story of its own and it's standing smack on Bar W property.'

'A ranch on a ranch?' Tony looked at Cal in amazement, but Laura didn't look at him because she suddenly knew what he was going to say.

'Blue Moon is not a ranch,' Cal said quietly. 'Charlie built it and he lived there. Josh spent plenty of time there too. But there is no ranch at all except the Bar W and it stretches as far as the eyes can see and more.'

They came to the top of the rise and looked down into the next small valley. 'That's Blue Moon,' Cal said. He pointed down to a log cabin set in a small paddock not much bigger than a good-sized lawn. The cabin was long and low, with two windows at the front and a small out-house standing at the back. There was a well at the side of the house, all fancied up like a well in a fairy tale. There had been an attempt to make the place look pretty but that was all.

'There's no running water,' Cal informed them quietly. 'There's no modern sanitation, no heating in the winter except a log fire. There's no land except what you can see inside the fence. That's all there is to Blue Moon.'

Laura couldn't speak. It would have been better if Cal had told them the night before that there was nothing at all because there really was nothing except this cabin planted on Wexford land. It seemed like a terribly cruel joke their father had played on them and she set off down the hill, trying to curb the tears that started hot and angry at the back of her eyes.

There was no Eldorado, there was just a log cabin with no land, and she had spent the better part of her savings to come here and claim what her father had left for them both. This was what he'd left. Now they had no home at all, nothing and nobody to go back to. She had foolishly left security and she didn't care for herself, but for Tony.

It was true she'd just taken a vacation from her job and she could go back to it, but how would they manage with just her job and no house, with Tony to go to university?

Tony started off after her but Cal grasped his arm.

'Let her be. We'll go down to her in a minute. She's got to get herself together first and she won't want us prying while she's upset.'

'It's all my fault,' Tony muttered. 'Laurie would never have come if it hadn't been for me. She thinks things through but I never gave her the chance to think. I'd almost got her convinced when Bruce Martin called and his attitude was enough to have her digging her heels in.' He swept his hand across his eyes, almost in tears. 'I know what she'll be doing right now. She'll be trying to make plans about how she's going to manage. God! I hate my father. How could he do this to her when she's always struggled to give me things? How could he just go off and leave her anyway? She's always been so bright and cheerful. She's lovely.'

Cal watched her walk down to the cabin. The sun was glinting on her long hair making it look like white gold.

She *was* lovely and it seemed she'd never been able to think of herself at all. He remembered Charlie, who hadn't had a care in the world because he'd refused any responsibility. Well, Charlie wasn't getting away with it this time.

'Let's go down and join her,' he said aloud. If he'd read her right she would have everything under nice tight control by now and he had a plan. He was banking on Laura's devotion to her brother. Maybe that made him a rogue too, but he was prepared to risk it.

He looked up at the cloudless sky. It was blue, endless, the gateway to heaven. If Charlie and Josh were angels up there he could guarantee they wouldn't last long. Maybe what he was about to do would wipe the smiles off their faces. He sure hoped so.

More than that he hoped Laura would agree to his plan. He was pretty certain of Tony, but, in spite of her delicate appearance, Laura was the power that held them afloat. Cal pulled a wry face. He had some fast talking to do and if he grinned once in the wrong place, he'd lose.

There were cattle milling round the fence and Cal scowled at them, waving his hands and giving a loud, high-pitched whistle that had them pulling back.

'They're not likely to do any damage here,' Laura said tightly.

'I'm more worried about them damaging themselves,' Cal muttered, glaring at them. 'This bit of grass is supposed to be kept short. It's too encouraging when it gets as high as this. When I came by this morning there were two steers with their heads fast in the fence. They're not too blessed with brainpower. They just go for what they want and right now they want the grass inside the fence just because it's not outside.'

Laura knew exactly why the two ranch hands had been

at the receiving end of his temper this morning. She could understand it now.

'Why don't you just pull the fence down?' she asked in a dull voice. Why hadn't he simply pulled the cabin down when her father had left?

'The fence isn't mine to touch. This was Charlie's place. He came up to Canada with money he'd earned in the oil fields and he managed to persuade Josh to let him buy this bit of the Bar W. He stayed on because he was happy here and the rest of the money he used up in drinking and gambling. Sometimes he was in funds and living high. Sometimes he was cleaned out and barely managing, but he always came around somehow.'

'He could have come home to England.'

'Yes, he could, I expect. He only went home when he knew he was dying. You never could fathom out how Charlie's mind worked.'

'It worked to his own advantage,' Laura snapped, turning away. 'Well, I suppose we own the fence and the cabin now, so you can get someone to pull both of them down as soon as you like.' She looked across the rolling acres of the Bar W. 'It's a bit like buying a pond in the sand at the edge of the ocean, isn't it? One good tide and it would all be swept away. I should have asked to see deeds but somehow I expected they would be here with your father. I think they expected that in Edmonton too. You could simply have pulled the lot down. It's on your land.'

'It's yours,' Cal reminded her quietly. 'I don't need to see deeds. I know how my father and Charlie worked.'

She turned to him with her face sad, a bittersweet smile touching her soft lips. 'Then we give it to you. It's for your kindness to us and payment for the bed and board. Just get us back to Leviston and we'll call it even.'

Before he could speak she walked to Tony, who was

standing leaning over the fence. She slid her arm in his and put her fair head against his tawny hair.

'Well,' she said softly, 'we had an adventure, didn't we? There never was any Eldorado but it was good while it lasted.'

'It's all my fault, Laurie. I should have listened to you when you had doubts.' Tony looked at her with real misery on his face but she shook her head and smiled.

'Shh. It was fun. Something to remember. We've seen a real ranch and met a real cowboy. I even saw him ride this morning, just like they do in the westerns. We'll go back home and start all over again.'

Tony threw his arm round her shoulders. 'You're wonderful, Laurie. You're the most wonderful person in the world, too good for Bland Bruce.'

Laura laughed. The tilted, dark eyes sparkled and the lovely face suddenly glowed. Cal hadn't managed to make her laugh but Tony had, and Cal was standing with his thumbs hooked in his pockets just watching her when she turned to him.

'We can go back now. Thank you for bringing us here and thank you for everything.' She smiled at him and Cal led them back up the hill to the pick-up. So far, so good. Now he had to make his plan work and he knew he would have to go easy. There was a pride about Laura that would refuse all help.

He'd been sitting at his desk for a good while last night and he thought he had it all worked out, but one mistake and they would be on their way. He didn't want that. There was something about Charlie's family that got under a man's skin—especially Laura. She was more than getting under his skin. He couldn't take his eyes from her and even when they were driving back he had to keep glancing at her. He couldn't help wishing that she'd rest her head on his shoulder again.

When they drove into the yard, Cal encouraged them to hang about and Tony didn't need encouragement. He was looking with eyes filled with longing at just about everything, and when a rider came into the yard and dismounted Cal had his chance.

'Let's see you ride that horse,' he ordered.

Tony spun round and stared at him. 'It belongs to that man who—'

'It's a Bar W horse. Strictly speaking it belongs to me, so go on. Walk across there, mount up and ride.'

Tony continued to stare at him in astonishment and Cal raised black brows.

'Chicken? I thought you had plans to be a rancher?'

Tony looked furious until he noticed that the blue eyes were gleaming with amusement and then he laughed.

'I'll do it! See if I don't.' He went off at a run and Laura gasped and moved forward.

'Tony!'

'Leave him be,' Cal ordered. 'Let's see if he can learn like I learned. I got thrown into the saddle and I had to ride or fall off.'

'You're a lot bigger than Tony,' Laura pointed out angrily.

He grinned. 'Sure I am and I'd like to see anybody throw me into the saddle now. But I was a baby when I was born and babies come small. That's how nature works.'

Laura glared up into the laughing eyes. 'It's not funny,' she snapped. 'He could be killed.'

'He's got more chance of being killed crossing the road in Edmonton.' He put his arm around her shoulders and pulled her close. 'Ease off. Let him have his thrill.'

'If you're suggesting that I mollycoddle him...' Laura began, struggling to get free.

Cal simply tightened his arm. 'I've no idea what that strange word means but if it means what I think it does then, yes, I think you're inclined to be a bit too ready to spoon-feed him. He's grown up. Let him be. Think about yourself for a change.'

'He's not grown up and it has nothing whatever to do with you,' she raged, struggling some more. 'Let me go at once!'

'No,' Cal said, holding her fast. 'You'd rush over there and spook the horse. Calm down, Laura. I've got it all in hand.'

'The only thing you've got in hand is me!'

Laura stood stiff as a poker and Cal grinned to himself, keeping a firm grip on her. He sure did have her in hand and he liked it just fine. Now let Tony ride—even a bit would do. He willed him up into the saddle and kept him there by sheer power of mind.

Tony was a natural. Even Laura could see that and her tight stance relaxed as he wheeled the horse around and trotted it about the yard. She tightened up a bit when he set it to the gallop but he managed that too.

Finally he trotted towards them grinning all over his face and dismounted with a flourish.

'That was some display for a first-time rider,' Cal said, and Laura could hear admiration in his voice.

'I've got a collection of old John Wayne movies.' Tony laughed. 'Bet I could round up the strays with no trouble and hog-tie a steer at round-up.'

'Well, you've got the vocabulary,' Cal said. He took a deep breath, still keeping his restraining grip on Laura. 'How would you like to work on the Bar W during your year off from university?'

'You—you're joking,' Tony said, looking excited all the same.

'I'm not joking. As far as I can see, you're both planning to go to England and work enough to get you right back where you were before you came out here. I'm offering you a job and the chance to learn what ranch life is like.'

Tony looked at Laura, not noticing the dismay in her eyes.

'I could work to get things back to normal, Laurie. You wouldn't have to be so worried about me. I'd have my own money to help out at university.'

'We'd be separated,' Laura whispered.

'Only if you want to be,' Cal said. He let her go and looked down at her seriously. 'I've got a job for you too. One that's needed doing for a good long while—too long.'

Laura looked desperate. 'But I can't do anything on a ranch.'

'According to Tiger here, you were a big-deal secretary.'

'I was PA to the managing director.'

'That sounds big-deal enough,' Cal said with mocking indulgence in his eyes. 'Come up to the house and we'll talk terms.'

He walked away and Laura found herself trotting after him, marshalling all her excuses and objections.

'I can't stay here. I've still got a job in England and if I stay here for a year I'll have to resign.'

'So resign,' he said, still striding off.

'Wait,' Laura ordered. 'I took a big chance coming out here and it was a mistake. I just can't put all our future into this. It's far too risky.'

Cal stopped and turned to face her. 'You don't trust me? Have I let you down so far?'

'I do trust you. How could I not? But you're doing this because you feel sorry for us.'

Cal's eyebrows rose. 'Wait until you see what I've got for you, lady. The favour will be all yours.'

He looked at Tony, who had tagged along watching them anxiously. 'You see that man who's just come into the yard?'

'Yes.' Tony looked across to where a tall man with long black hair was unsaddling a horse.

'Blackfoot,' Cal said. 'His name is Michael Silver. He's been on the ranch since I was a boy. We grew up together. Frank Alders is the foreman but Mike knows more about horses than anyone I've ever met. He taught me all the tricks and he'll teach you if he likes you. Go and speak to him.'

'He might not like me.'

'Tell him I sent you. Tell him your name is Tiger and tell him Charlie was your father.'

'That'll put him off,' Tony muttered.

'I doubt it. Charlie once saved his life. Come along, Laura. I hope you're going to accept this job because I'm just about at my wits' end.'

Tony went off readily enough and Laura turned back to the house. 'I know you're lying but I'll come.' She sighed.

'Now why should I be lying?'

'Because, as far as I can tell, you've got more wits than any three other men. You're not likely to be at the end of them.'

He grinned down at her. 'You're not as fragile as you look, are you?'

'I'm not fragile at all,' Laura said crossly. 'But if what you really mean is that I'm stupid, then I agree with you. I was stupid to get us into this mess and I'm just stupid enough to hope we can get out of it and still stay in this beautiful place.'

'You can. You can even stay in the house.'

'Why?' Laura asked. 'Why, why, why?'

'Well,' he confessed. 'I can't give Charlie a swift kick in the pants, him being out of my reach, so this is one way to get back at him.'

'Did you dislike my father so much?' Laura asked as they went up the steps of the house.

He gave a hard laugh. 'Maybe I should have done. But somehow I never got around to it. Charlie was a law until himself. Everybody grumbled about him, especially when he took them for their week's wages at poker, but everybody liked him. Besides,' he added, slanting her another look as blue as the sky, 'I like you and Tony.'

'I like you too and I'm sure Tony does.'

'So where are the snags?'

'I haven't found any yet but I'm still looking.'

'Maybe you'll pine for Bland Bruce?'

Laura glared at him. 'That's most unlikely. He was one of the reasons I agreed to this hare-brained scheme.'

Cal looked innocently surprised. 'It wasn't hare-brained.'

'We'll see,' Laura promised darkly. 'And I warn you, I'm a stubborn, autocratic PA.'

'Just what I need.' Cal grinned, ushering her into the house. 'I've had things all my own way for far too long.'

The place where Cal worked on his papers was a study off the hall. Cal called it his office and when they walked into it Laura was stunned at the chaos. She was accustomed to order, routine and systematically assigning things to their correct place. In any case, this whole house was gleamingly beautiful.

Cal worked in total disorder. After she'd seen the neat buildings of the ranch and the smooth running of everything, his office came as a shock. She just stood and looked around in bewilderment.

'Bad, huh?' Cal muttered. 'There's a lot of paperwork to

running a spread this size. I've got too much to do to deal with it. It gets all over.'

'Only because you let it get all over,' Laura pointed out. 'You've got a computer. Why don't you use that?'

'I don't trust it.' Cal scowled at the gleaming machine that sat by itself on a table at the side of the room. 'I like things in my hands. They disappear when you shut that thing off and I never expect to see them again.'

Laura found herself grinning. For such a big, competent man he seemed downright scared of a little machine that would have saved him from all this.

'Everyone to his own trade,' she said brightly. 'You deal with the ranch and I'll deal with the paperwork.'

'You'll stay?' He looked stunned at her acceptance.

'How could I refuse? You've been so good to us, Tony has his dream and it's obvious that you need help.'

Cal narrowed his eyes and pulled a sinister face. 'How do you know I didn't come in here last night and toss things around a bit?'

'Well, in the first place you wouldn't be so idiotic, and in the second place there's a certain order to the chaos. It looks as if a well-planned bomb hit it.'

Cal put his hands on her shoulders and looked down at her. 'I don't want you to do this for me because of any feeling of gratitude. I don't want you to do this for Tony either. I want you to stay because you really want to stay.'

Laura looked up at him. She felt surprisingly comfortable with his hands on her shoulders. She felt warm and safe. Almost since the first moment she had seen Cal she'd felt safe. She normally took a long time to trust anyone but she trusted this tall man with black hair and blue eyes. Once again she felt she was drowning.

She looked away quickly. 'I really want to stay. I don't

often get the chance to have my cake and eat it too. This is a perfect place, a dream place.'

'You mean my office?'

He was back to being amused and Laura felt the exciting tension leave her in a rush. If she could just curb this desire to watch him and hang onto his every word she would be all right.

'It will be when I've sorted it out.' She became very businesslike. 'What's in the filing cabinets?'

Cal looked wary again. 'More papers. Want to resign?'

Laura walked across and opened the drawers, her eyebrows shooting up at what she saw. 'If I resign you'll have to get someone in. This lot will eventually attack you.'

'I don't want anyone in but you,' Cal said stubbornly. 'I already told you I don't like people in the house.'

Laura looked at him in amusement. 'I'm people.'

'You're different. I like having you around.'

'The novelty of the unexpected,' Laura murmured.

'Don't sound so sulky. Let's have some coffee and then I'll have to leave you. I've got to see that Tiger is settled with Mike and then I've got to take a couple of the boys and inspect the fences a few miles off. Some of them were looking pretty soggy when I rode round this morning. I don't want cattle getting into the wheat and I don't want them getting fast in Charlie's excuse for a fence either.'

He walked out into the hall, back to business with a vengeance, and Laura followed, feeling that she'd just spent a little while out of time. She had the sudden urge to beg to go with him but she quelled that firmly. She had a job, a beautiful house to live in and when they went to England she would have enough money to start afresh. Somehow, the latter idea didn't seem as bright as it should have done.

*   *   *

Laura decided to start as soon as Cal rode off. She could see Tony in the yard with Michael Silver. He was learning how to saddle a horse. For once, she had no responsibilities weighing her down. She just had to make order appear out of chaos.

When she went to get changed she found that everything was creased and she rushed down to consult Biddy, who was in the kitchen.

'Sure we've got an ironing-board and an iron,' Biddy said. 'But don't you bother. I'll get your things and do them.'

'I couldn't ask you to do that. You've got far too much to do as it is.'

'It's easy here. Two of the other wives help out twice a week and Marge brings her own ironing-board and iron. We put them in the kitchen facing each other and talk like mad. You leave your things to me. We'll get them done this afternoon, Tony's too.'

Better and better, Laura thought as she went back to her room. She hated ironing in any case, and now she could get right down to work, although she had intended to dress in something suitable. That office needed a disciplined approach; it probably needed a dark dress and a sour attitude. It would have to make do with jeans and a red shirt.

She braided her thick hair as she did for work and went down to show it who was boss.

It was getting dark when Cal finally came in and Laura was still hard at it. He came into the office when he couldn't find her anywhere else.

'You've got to stop,' he ordered. 'I planned on this taking you a whole year. If you get it done sooner I'll have to ask you to clean out the stables.'

He looked round in surprise at the order she was creating.

'You threw out some papers?'

'I filed them until I could speak to you. I fed plenty of them into the computer first.'

'It chewed them up?' Cal looked uneasy about it and she had to laugh at his expression.

'Of course it didn't. When you've got time, I'll show you how it works.'

'I don't want to know. I'm too busy to work in here.'

Laura looked at him with severity. 'You'll have to know for when I'm gone.'

'You're not going. Obviously you belong here. I aim to keep you.'

Laura laughed. 'How can you be so afraid of a little computer? You're probably doing dangerous things all day. The computer is harmless.'

'It's a monster. You'll control it.' He walked across to her and looked at her hair. 'You look different, efficient.'

'I probably scared the papers and the computer.'

'No. You look good.' He put his hand out and gave a little tug at her thick braid. 'Mike's hair never looks as good as this and he's always got his hair tied back. Not so elaborate, though, and not so pretty.' He laughed when her face flushed. 'He never blushes either. Mind you, I never tell him he's pretty.'

When she looked absolutely confused he put his arm round her shoulders. 'Come on. We'll get ready to eat. I probably smell like a steer and you look tired.'

'I'm not a bit tired,' Laura protested, wanting to snuggle against him.

'I warned you. Finish too soon and I'll make you clean the stables.'

'I can go home when it's all finished,' Laura quipped, thinking she was entering into the spirit of things.

He stopped in the hall and looked down at her. 'It's a

long walk to Leviston. You can't ride a horse so you must be planning to steal the Chevy.'

'I was joking,' Laura said, looking up at him, and he tilted her face with one brown hand.

'You'd better be. I went to a whole lot of trouble to get you and I'll probably tie you to that computer if you try to leave.'

'I'm kidnapped?' She still smiled up at him and his eyes roamed over her face.

'That's about the size of it,' he said softly. 'This is a big ranch and I'm king of the castle out here. I told you I'd had my own way for far too long. I'm not used to rebellion, so don't rebel.'

The smile died on Laura's face. 'I know you're joking, but you might like to know that you're frightening me.'

She got his usual long, slow grin. 'Now why would I do that? You're my new PA.'

Laura found that her ironing had been done and all the clothes hung nicely. She had a shower and changed and when she got downstairs she found that Cal had changed too. He was wearing dark trousers and a dark shirt.

He shot a quick look at her and poured her a drink. She had a white, silky dress on now and her hair was freshly washed and brushed until it shone.

The atmosphere was a bit tight and she looked round for Tony, hoping he'd give her some support. She was still feeling a bit of the shivery excitement that Cal's words had provoked earlier.

'Tony's eating with the other hands in the cookhouse,' he said when he noticed her anxious glances. 'Apparently he doesn't do things by halves. He's really taken to Mike and he feels that if he's trying to be a ranch hand he'd better act like one all the time.'

'I suppose that's a good idea,' Laura said dubiously.

'Are you worried about him?'

'No. I know where he is.'

Cal frowned but said nothing as Biddy came in with the meal. Laura was glad to see her.

'Thank you for doing my ironing, Biddy,' she said, smiling at the woman. 'I hate ironing.'

'Better than working in that office,' Biddy said with a disapproving sniff. 'Haven't been able to dust in there for ages. When you've got it all sorted, I'll tackle it.'

'What will you do if Tony decides to live in the quarters?' Cal asked when Biddy had bustled out of the room.

'What should I do? When he's at university I'll not be able to keep an eye on him.'

'He doesn't need anyone to keep an eye on him,' Cal snapped. 'He's almost a man.'

'But not quite,' Laura reminded him, temper showing in her eyes.

He looked at her steadily. 'Quite the little wildcat when Tony comes into the equation, aren't you? You're efficient in the office, quiet and gentle on other occasions, but let anything threaten Tony and you're ready to do battle.'

'I've been looking after Tony for too long to just ignore his best interests,' Laura flared.

Cal just got on with his meal and didn't look up. 'Are you certain you know what his best interests are?'

'You think you know better than I do? You don't know us at all.' Laura felt miserable that they seemed to be quarrelling, but she wouldn't let it pass. She couldn't let it pass. She was too used to being Tony's lifeline.

'I know you.' Cal looked up at her, ignoring her obvious rage. 'What I didn't know from observation, Tony told me.'

'You encouraged him to talk about me?' Laura looked outraged.

'He doesn't need any encouragement. He thinks you're

the bee's knees. If anyone so much as looks at you sideways I'm expecting to have to separate them from a big fight because, even if Tony comes off worst, he'll go for their throats.'

'We've been alone for so long,' Laura said more quietly. 'Even when my mother was alive we were really alone because she was always grumbling about Dad when she could so easily have divorced him and found someone else.'

'Maybe she didn't want to find someone else,' Cal suggested.

'He obviously never intended to come back.'

'I didn't mean she was waiting for him, longing for his return. I mean she probably had things just as she liked them. Two kids to complain to and no man in the house.'

Laura nodded. 'That's what Tony thinks.'

'It makes sense. Some people are like that.'

'You're thinking about yourself and the way you don't like visitors?'

'Who said I didn't like visitors? I just don't like having household staff underfoot every day.'

'I'll be underfoot,' Laura pointed out.

'I've never noticed you being underfoot,' Cal said quietly. 'Besides, I chose to have you here.'

CHAPTER FOUR

CAL went on eating and so did Laura. There was a provocative silence. It seemed to be swirling in the air, almost choking her.

'I suppose it was hard when you had the whole ranch to care for and were still really only a boy,' she ventured finally.

Cal gave a short laugh. 'I'm not sure if I ever was a boy. I never noticed if it was hard either. I went off to college when I was about Tony's age because it was something I felt I had to do. That was a big mistake. When I came back the whole place was in a turmoil. If it hadn't been for Frank Alders and Mike, I doubt if there would have been anything left. Josh had taken charge and messed up just about everything. I never did finish college.'

'I'm sorry. I suppose you missed out.'

He shot a quick look at her. 'I imagined that at the time but, after all, I would have come back here and been doing exactly what I'm doing now.' He smiled. 'Maybe I would have learned to trust a computer but I can't think of any other thing I missed.'

When Laura was silent, thinking her own thoughts, Cal watched the light gleaming on her hair and the velvet skin of her face. She drew him like a magnet without doing anything at all. He wanted to hold her close and nibble at her. Just about anywhere would do.

'We'll have coffee in the other room,' he said, helping her to her feet. 'Biddy serves coffee and then she goes.'

The other room was a huge sitting room with paintings of horses, the ranch and the Rocky Mountains on the walls. Like everywhere else in the house it was luxurious, and when they'd finished their coffee Cal took her hand and led her to the window.

He put the outside lights on and pointed to the wall that swept round the side. 'You see that wall? Sometimes the snow comes more than halfway up in winter. There'll come a morning when I wake up and it's so quiet, so bright that I know. And I'm wondering if the cattle are lost in the drifts. I'm wondering if they'll all survive and there's nothing I can do about it until the boys come and we've dug a way out and ploughed a road to go and look for them.' He was silent for a while and then he said, 'At night I come back here and the house is quiet, really quiet. There's nothing to hear except the snow cracking on the roof and the odd call of a deer. There's just silence.'

Foolishly she wanted to comfort him. He wasn't the sort of man who needed comforting, but she wanted to go close to him and say, 'I'll be here when the snow comes. It won't be silent.'

Of course he spoiled it all by grinning down at her serious face and saying, 'Sorry for me?'

She shot him an outraged look. 'Were you trying to invoke my sympathy?'

'Sure. Nearly got to you there, didn't I?' He stared into her eyes until she laughed and nodded.

'I was all ready to promise to take care of you.'

Cal ran his fingers down her face. 'You don't need to take care of me. I've been taking care of everyone else for years. Just promise to be here when the first snow comes. You'll never see a more beautiful sight. I want to show you the trees with snow falling from their branches, the hills with a white covering like fairyland.'

'And the cattle caught in a snowdrift,' she said, smiling up at him.

'You'll only see that if we get short-handed. Before winter comes, I'll teach you to ride.'

Laura's face lit up and he grinned at her.

'I hope you studied those old John Wayne movies with Tony.'

Later, the storm that had been threatening for two days broke over the ranch house like a vicious animal in a rage. The wind howled and the rain hit the windows like bullets. Laura had never felt so much at the mercy of the elements before and she wondered what it would be like here in winter.

The front door banged and Tony seemed to shoot into the house on the wind. Laura went out of her room and looked down over the balustrade in time to see Cal go into the hall to greet her brother.

'Wow! Thought I'd never make it across the yard,' Tony said, laughing all over his face.

'This is just an itty-bitty storm,' Cal jeered. 'Wait until you face a real one.' He was grinning at her brother and Laura watched them from the stairs. 'How did it go?' Cal asked quietly.

'Great! I enjoyed myself. I could really take to this life.'

'Wait until you've ridden all day and can't get out of the saddle, then tell me.'

'Mike already warned me about that. He gave me a few tips.'

Cal burst into laughter. 'Frank gave me a few tips too when I started, but I was still bow-legged for a month.'

'I'll chance it,' Tony laughed and then said seriously, 'There was a good meal in the cookhouse and I've been thinking, if I'm going to do this right, maybe I ought to sleep over there like everyone else does.'

'Sure, whatever you like.'

They both glanced up as Laura made her way down the stairs and Tony looked guilty.

'Laurie, I've just been suggesting—' Tony began.

'I heard you. I was spying from the top of the stairs. If you're going to be a ranch hand, don't mind me. I work in the house—it's cleaner.' She cast a dubious glance at his appearance and he brightened.

'I know how I look—I've been with Mike amongst the horses all day. I've got to take a hot shower and then I'm just going to fall into bed.' He grinned at her. 'It was great.'

Laura watched him pound up the stairs. Without any effort, her brother was pulling away from her and she had mixed feelings about that. She was proud of him, relieved in a way that he was standing alone and determined to succeed. She could see a time in the future when he would want to stay here and not go back with her. That made her feel a little lost.

Cal took her arm. 'Come in here and I'll pour you a night-time drink. You did that very well. I'm filled with admiration.'

'He wanted us to fly free. That's what he said to convince me to come here. Now he's flying free without me and it only took two days.'

'I know it's hard when you've done everything for him. You've been big sister for too long.'

Laura gave a short laugh and turned away. 'I suppose I feel left out. I've had nothing on my mind but looking after

Tony for so many years that I'm a little scared now he's pulling free.'

'Finally he would pull free altogether wherever you were. Just allow him some slack. You're not going to lose him. But he's almost a man now.'

'I know. But it's scary. I feel like somebody who's been dropped overboard.'

He turned her to face him. 'You'll not go under. I won't let you.' He was looking into her eyes and Laura didn't feel quite so sad. She smiled.

'About that. I can't swim either,' she confessed.

'Hell! You're going to take up a lot of my time. I should take on an extra foreman and devote all my spare hours to you.' He touched her face and she felt the fire springing from his fingertips again, warming her all over. 'Maybe I'll do that,' he added softly. 'I always wanted a hobby.'

When she went on looking at him he leaned forward and touched his lips to hers. It was nothing more than a gentle salute but it felt wonderful. Laura closed her eyes and forgot to be wary and scared.

He lifted his head and saw her closed eyes and the expression on her face. Then he kissed her again, deepening the kiss until stars seemed to be dancing all over her.

It backfired mightily. Cal didn't even know if he could stop. He just wanted to go on and on devouring her. She tasted so sweet that he simply wanted to gobble her up and never stop at all.

When he let her go and she opened her eyes, he was staring at her as if he'd had as much of a shock as she had.

'I think we'll forget about the drink,' he said in an abrupt voice. 'I think you'd be better in bed. It's safer. When you get up in the morning, I'll be long gone. I guess it's time this ranch returned to normal. Normal is when I work all day. I'll see you at dinner.'

'All right. I'll have plenty to do.'

She walked out on trembling legs and Cal ran his hand through his thick hair when the door closed behind her. He'd wanted to take that kiss a whole lot further. He'd wanted to lash his arms round her and let nature take its course.

He poured the drink for himself, a stiff one. 'Hell and damnation,' he muttered. 'I'm not cut out to be a saint after all.'

Gradually, Laura brought order to the chaos in Cal's study. She arranged a filing system for him and then continued to feed things into the computer. She learned a lot while she was doing it too. This ranch was big, seventy thousand acres, a size her mind couldn't quite take in. There was pasture and wheat and over five thousand head of cattle at the last count.

She filed bills of sale, veterinary reports and grain returns. The bills that needed paying she put on his desk. There were not many of those. This ranch was rich and so was Cal Wexford. In England he would have been a big landowner. Here, he just acted like a cowboy.

She didn't see much of him now because he was gone in the morning and sometimes he didn't even return for dinner. Biddy explained it all.

'The boys will be busy from morning to night at the moment,' she said. 'When the winter hits us we'll want everything settled and safe. We could lose a good few head of cattle if the winter's bad.'

'Is it always bad?'

'Mostly, but we have the chinook here and that brings a

soft feel to the air when it blows. This is the sunshine state. In many ways we're lucky.'

After dinner, which Laura ate alone, she went back to the office and worked. She was living in what amounted to luxury but she was getting more lonely every day and winter wasn't here yet. She hardly ever saw Cal.

He walked in when she least expected it and he looked tired. He dropped into a big chair by the fireplace and closed his eyes for a minute.

'You look tired out,' Laura said when he just sat there with his eyes closed.

He nodded, looking across at her as she sat at his desk. 'I am tired. I'm running myself and everybody else ragged.'

'Biddy told me how much work you have to do before winter sets in. I've been filing papers and reading them. I realise how much you have to do.'

He hooked a leg over the side of the chair. 'Do you? I knew you'd be indispensable. Pretty soon I'm going to be asking you what to do every day.'

Laura smiled. 'Don't worry. I won't get around to that. But by the time I go, I can guarantee you'll have everything in order here.'

Cal watched her steadily. 'Stop threatening me. You're not going.'

'I won't leave and pitch you back into turmoil. Everything will be done before I go and I'm hoping to introduce you to the computer.' He didn't say anything and Laura began to feel uneasy. 'I suppose I should get to bed now,' she murmured.

When he didn't reply she packed up the papers she was working on and set off for the door. He was giving off feelings she didn't understand, but she knew he was either annoyed about something or planning something.

As she was passing his chair he stretched out his hand and captured her wrist.

'Been lonely?' he asked, looking up at her.

'A little,' she confessed. 'When Biddy isn't here it's very quiet in the house.'

'Then why haven't you asked to come out with me?'

Laura stared down at him in surprise. 'But I didn't know I could ask. You're so busy and I would be in the way. I sometimes see Tony crossing the yard but he always looks as if he's running.'

'Ah! It's Tony you're missing.'

'I never said that,' Laura protested. 'Stop putting words into my mouth. I only said that it's quiet when you're not here and I'm sometimes lonely.'

He uncoiled himself from the chair without letting go of her wrist. When he stood she found herself very close to the hard wall of his chest.

'Then come with me tomorrow,' he said quietly. 'There's more to a ranch than papers. Tomorrow you'll ride with the boss. One short lesson is all you get, then you tag along with me.'

'I'll never keep up with you.' Laura's face had lit up with surprise and excitement and he looked down at her and smiled.

'Then I'll just haul you onto my horse and we'll jog along like that.' He looked into her smiling face, his eyes roaming over it and his own face softening.

'So did you miss me?' He looked at her through his lashes and Laura felt quite defiant.

'Yes,' she said tartly. 'I missed you. I was hoping to see you terrified by that computer.'

When he just grinned she broke his grip on her wrist and

then sat down in another chair by the fireplace, facing him with a determined look on her face.

'You'll have to learn it.'

'What?' He looked innocently mystified, another way he had of teasing. Laura ignored it.

'You'll have to learn to use the computer. Why did you buy it if it's to be left sitting there unused?'

Cal looked disgusted. 'Josh bought it. It was another of his bright ideas.'

'Then he could use it?'

'Of course he couldn't. I was the one expected to learn. I had too much to do as it was. Besides,' he added, looking like a resentful schoolboy, 'I hated to do any of the crazy things he suggested.'

'Oh, you were unhappy.' Laura touched his hand. 'I'm sorry.'

Before she could move her hand he'd captured it and she found herself looking into laughing eyes. 'Oh, I'm getting the hang of you, Laura Hughes,' he said. 'You're bad-tempered but you're soft-hearted.'

'I'm not a bit soft-hearted.'

'Yes, you are. You're a sweetheart with hair like moon-light. I can get round you with no trouble at all.' He let her hand go. 'I'll come back for you after breakfast and we'll have you riding before the day is over.'

'Do you think I'll be able to do it?'

'Absolutely. It's necessary here and you'll be here for ages—maybe years.'

'I won't be here for years,' Laura said. She didn't know it but she sounded rather sombre. Her face looked wistful.

'Want to bet?' he asked.

When she went to bed, Laura was almost too excited to sleep and it wasn't only the thought of going out in the morning. It was the thought of going out with Cal. He had made her feel excited from the moment she'd seen him and now she looked for him coming home every day, bitterly disappointed when he didn't arrive. For the first time in her life she was dreaming, dreaming of the kiss he'd given her.

Of course he'd pulled back rapidly and then he'd stayed away every day. But now she was going out with him to-morrow and she was looking forward to it so much that she almost forgot she would have to ride.

Next morning, when she presented herself in the yard, dressed in jeans and a dark green shirt, she was dismayed to find several ranch hands were there also. They were re-ceiving their orders from Cal and Frank and when they saw her they obviously wanted to hang around.

'Mount up and get moving,' Cal ordered when he noticed their interest in her. 'Look too hard at her and Tiger will be starting a fight. If he doesn't bloody your noses, I will.'

They grinned cheerfully and moved off, touching their hats to Laura in a way she found charming.

'Oh, aren't they nice?' she whispered to Cal.

He looked at her askance, his eyebrows raised. 'Yeah, very nice,' he said sarcastically. 'Come on Red Riding Hood. Let's get out of here before the wolves eat you.'

'I'm sure they're not wolves.'

'Well, let's just say that they're not about to get the chance to prove that one way or the other. You've got three knights to defend you: Tiger, Frank and me.'

'Don't forget Mike.' Frank laughed. 'He's a mean fighter.'

'Too mean,' Cal muttered. 'I wouldn't wish Mike on my worst enemy.'

'You wished him on Tony,' Laura ventured, and when Cal rolled his eyes heavenward Frank chuckled.

'Tony's not a pretty lady, ma'am. There's a shortage of beautiful women on the Bar W.'

'I'll mention that to Biddy,' Laura said smartly and Cal threw his head back and laughed.

'Better move out, Frank. She's as sharp as a needle. I think she could take care of herself in any case.'

As Frank rode off, still laughing, Cal brought a saddled horse up and walked it around in front of her.

'Let her see you and come closer,' he said. 'Touch her and don't be afraid. That will make her uneasy.'

'I'm not afraid. She's beautiful. Does she have a name?'

'They all have names. This one is Sky. Don't know how she got that name but she's gentle and well-mannered. She's not fast but she's sturdy.'

Laura stroked the soft nose and let Sky sniff at her hand. She ran her fingers down the horse's silky neck and her smile grew by the minute.

'Hi, sis!' Tony came out of one of the barns and almost made her jump. Sis! That was something he hadn't said before. He called in to see her every day but he was totally embroiled in the ranch and his determination to be a cowboy.

Michael Silver came out slowly too. It was the first time Laura had seen him close up and she found herself looking into eyes much darker than her own. He was about Cal's age, maybe just younger, and in a way he was quite beautiful. His skin was golden and his hair was heavy and black, beyond his shoulders and tied back as Cal had told her. He nodded to her. He was polite but didn't show any of the exuberance the others had done.

'Mike picked out the horse for you,' Tony said. 'The

boss has been really busy this morning. He had to work in some time to get you riding.'

'Remind me to thank you for that remark, Tiger. Get him cleaning saddles, Mike. I don't want him here giving Laura the benefit of his expertise.'

Mike smiled and put his hand on Tony's shoulder and Laura wondered if he ever spoke. He seemed to read her mind.

'Tiger never stops talking,' he said, his dark eyes flashing with amusement. 'All I've got to do is listen.'

When they walked off, Laura turned to Cal. 'How did he know what I was thinking?' she muttered in astonishment.

'Well, I could say it was an old Indian trick, but even a placid man like me could see what you're thinking. Everything shows on your face in large letters. Now the boys will have gone off thinking how nice they are. They'll be a whole bunch of trouble from now on.'

She looked a bit worried and he came round the horse to help her up into the saddle.

'Ease off, enjoy yourself and we'll ride away before any more people come riding up to look at you.'

'I'd rather be alone in case I fall off,' Laura said, looking at the horse with misgivings now.

'You're not going to fall off. Just let me know when you've had enough and I'll lift you off.'

It was surprisingly easy to mount the horse and easy enough to move forward. Out of the corners of her eyes she could see Tony and Mike watching from the door of the barn, and when Cal swung up onto his own horse she felt very proud of herself.

'Okay,' he said. 'Let's go while you're still up there.'

They rode through the trees behind the house and towards the low hills that climbed to the Rockies, but soon they turned onto the pastures that spread almost endlessly into the distance.

'Can't we ride into the hills?' Laura looked back as they turned onto the flatter plains.

'It's too difficult for a first-time rider. You'd have a lot of guiding to do. Here, the horse can make her own way. Besides, we don't want to meet a grizzly.'

'Could we?' Laura looked at him, her dark eyes like saucers.

He grinned at her apprehension. 'It's not very likely. They're shy creatures and keep out of the way but they're up there and they're not cuddly teddy bears.'

'I know,' Laura told him seriously. 'They're dangerous. Do they ever come down to the ranch?'

'Rarely. They don't like people. If they come down it's because they're hungry, but, like all bears, they sleep in the winter. You've got to be pretty stupid to get yourself into trouble with them. Campers and hikers who go unprepared up into the Rockies have narrow escapes sometimes.' He pushed his hat to the back of his head and smiled reminiscently. 'The sort of people who go fishing in the mountain lakes sometimes meet up with them.'

Laura glanced across at him. 'I suppose you mean like my father and yours?'

'They once met a grizzly at close quarters when they were fishing,' Cal said, his smile widening. 'It nearly scared their pants off.'

'What did they do?'

'They got on their horses and rode like the devil. Left all their fishing tackle behind and rode to the ranch as if they'd encountered an alien from outer space.'

Laura laughed at the picture he drew. 'So they lost their fishing gear?'

'Not so you'd notice. Of course, they wouldn't go back to get it. Mike and I went next morning and never even saw grizzly tracks. We thought about tearing our shirts and describing an attack but it wasn't worth the hassle. Charlie and Josh fished lower down after that.'

'You liked them both, didn't you?' Laura asked and he shot her a quick glance.

'I suppose so. How did you figure that out?'

'You speak about them as if they were children. You have a very indulgent way of speaking when you mention them.'

'You're not so easy to fool, are you? Yes, I suppose I felt indulgent when I got older. I suppose I understood them. In any case, I'm not given to keeping up resentment. It would only make me bitter. Josh never got over losing my mother and as to Charlie, well, he never did grow up.'

Laura was silent, wishing she had known these two characters who had caused mayhem and laughter. Fun had been a missing commodity in her own home and, since her mother died, Laura had been too concerned with juggling to make ends meet to think of fun.

It was so different here. Things just happened with a clockwork regularity. There was work to do. There was the feeling of being part of the earth and sky. It was impossible to step out of the house without feeling nature all around.

She sighed and looked up at the wide blue sky, the distant Rockies and the endless, rolling plains and Cal glanced across at her.

'Why the big sigh? Are you tired?'

Laura smiled and shook her head. 'No. I suppose I was dreaming. I haven't had much experience of dreaming but this place just lends itself to dreams. I think it's the sky and the mountains, the utter silence. It just makes all worries drop away.'

After a good while, when she was moving contentedly to the rhythm of the horse, Cal said, 'Let's make a stop here. We've come a long way and you'll feel the effect when you get down.'

They stopped by the trees and Cal came to help her down; he ended up lifting her out of the saddle. 'I can guarantee, no big, ferocious bear,' he said when her feet touched the ground.

'What would you do if we saw one?' She looked up at him as he stood with his arms still around her.

'Ride off and leave you. I'd be up in the saddle and away the moment I smelled danger.'

Laura smiled. 'I know you wouldn't.'

'No, I wouldn't.' He looked down into her eyes and when she went on looking at him he folded her completely into his arms and kissed her slowly and deeply.

Laura just closed her eyes and sank against him, glorying in the feeling that swept over her. She felt touched by stars again, by magic, and she had no thought in her head of pulling away. She was safe in the strong arms, lost in another place, more happy at that moment than she had ever been. The kiss went on and on until the horse moved impatiently.

Cal lifted his head when he felt the horse move. 'She doesn't like this,' he whispered against Laura's ear. 'Let's move before she gets jumpy.'

He led her to the grass under the trees and pulled her down beside him. They looked at each other for a second, and when she moved straight into his arms again Cal smiled

and cupped her head in his hands, looking down at her for
a long time.

'Pretty Laura. Sweet Laura. I wanted to kiss you the first
time I saw you,' he said quietly. 'I wanted to lift you up
and hug you. Would you have got back on the first train
out?'

'I suppose so,' she agreed in a trembling voice.

'I'm frightening you now?'

She shook her head, just looking at him, sinking into the
blue of his eyes.

'I'm frightening myself,' he muttered. 'Do you know
I've been driving everyone on this place like a madman,
just to keep away from you? I had to get myself so tired
that I was too exhausted to think.'

'I missed you,' Laura whispered.

She leaned forward and impetuously kissed his face and
he clutched her to him then, kissing her in a frenzy of
passion she didn't expect. She was on her back, Cal leaning
over her, and she could feel the leashed-in power of him.
She suddenly knew that if that power was ever unleashed
she would just go wherever he led.

She had never tempted this fall of fire before, had never
even known it existed. She had shuddered when she'd
thought of Bruce giving her a lover's kiss but she hadn't
really known what that was like. Now she wanted to know
more with an urgency that couldn't be denied. She kissed
him back recklessly and his response made them both trem-
ble. There was a driving energy about him that made her
limbs turn to water. Everything inside her felt soft and giving.

When Cal lifted his head and drew back to look at her
she was flushed and breathless. Her breasts were straining
against her shirt, the peaks tight and hard, tempting him.

His own breath was almost a gasp and he wanted to take her there and then.

He rolled off her, sitting up, taking deep, steadying breaths. Everything inside him wanted what she had so innocently offered.

After a moment he looked at her as she lay in the grass, her eyes still closed. She was lying quite still, her cheeks pink as a rose, her lips red and swollen from his kisses and her glorious hair spread around her head like a burst of winter sunlight. His eyes roamed over her and then he said, 'We'd better go back. You've had more than either of us bargained for.' She opened her eyes and he was looking down at her ruefully. 'I never intended to get you into this situation,' he confessed, 'but you pack more of a punch than I expected.'

When she looked slightly embarrassed, Cal sprang to his feet and pulled her up. 'Don't start looking like that,' he ordered. 'You look guilty. I'm the one who should be feeling the guilt—but I refuse to be sorry about something that took my breath away.'

Laura turned and began to walk back to where Sky was quietly grazing. She felt tremblingly aware of herself, tremblingly aware of Cal. She didn't know what to do or what to say because she'd never been in this situation before. She felt a sharp stab of guilt because she was sure she'd caused it all in the first place and telling herself that it just wasn't true didn't help much.

She need not have worried. Cal was back in control. When she came to Sky he took the reins and turned the horse for her to mount. This time, though, it wasn't so easy and Laura's face showed it.

'Saddle weary,' Cal observed when she pulled a face and

sat resolutely in the saddle. 'Mike has a magic ointment that he massages in when this happens.'

'He's not massaging anything into me,' Laura assured him indignantly, forgetting her embarrassment. 'It's not my shoulders that hurt.'

Cal laughed and swung onto his horse with an ease that made Laura glare. At the moment she didn't feel shocked at herself for responding to him in what she knew had been an abandoned manner. All she could think about was the way she felt sore all over and the way Cal was sitting so easily in the saddle, watching her.

'I could sit you up in front of me,' he offered, and she just knew he was stifling one of those long grins.

'No way,' she snapped. 'I'm not riding into the yard while all the ranch hands watch me and giggle about my predicament!'

'They wouldn't giggle,' Cal assured her, unable to keep the laughter from his face any longer. 'They just don't *do* that.'

'Then they'd go into the cookhouse and laugh their socks off,' Laura grumbled. 'I'll manage, thank you.'

'Okay. We'll ride but we won't whistle.' Cal turned his horse and they moved off slowly, Laura cringing at every step that Sky took.

After a while, Cal reined in and brought his horse close. 'Let me carry you in front of me,' he said softly. 'This is my fault. I should never have brought you so far on your first trip out. I wanted to get you to myself and all I've done is hurt you.'

'You didn't hurt me. I didn't hurt until I got off the horse.'

Cal grimaced. 'Ouch! That sounds like a double-edged statement.'

'It wasn't meant to be. I only meant that I didn't realise how stiff I'd be once I got down.' She turned to look at him in slight desperation. 'Can I ride with you on your horse? I'm not sure if I can make it as things are.'

He lifted her in front of him. He was very gentle and she just seemed to float across to him.

'Better?'

'Yes, thank you.' It would have been better still if she could have leaned on him but Laura sat like a ramrod, worried that she would be inviting more passion if she leaned back.

'Relax,' he said quietly. 'Nothing much can happen to you on a horse.'

'Please, don't,' Laura begged. 'You make me feel guilty about the way I behaved.'

Cal drew her back against him, settling her comfortably. 'There's no need to feel guilty,' he said. 'I had every intention of kissing you. I didn't realise what would happen when I got my hands on you. I didn't know I'd have trouble stopping. I'm taking you back for your own good, not for mine.'

CHAPTER FIVE

'I've never felt like that before,' Laura confessed quietly.

'I know. It dawned on me gradually. What's wrong with this Bruce character?'

'I think he was my mother's choice. He seemed to talk to her mostly when he called for me. He liked to be domineering. He liked to have his opinion sought about everything. He made me feel old. I'm not sure why I put up with it.'

She was sure really. She had been completely overwhelmed by her responsibilities but she felt so different now. Laura gave a big sigh and looked round at the hills and the sky, at the drifting cattle and the trees. The sun was shining on everything and a breeze blew gently. There was so much silence, so much peace.

'It's quite wonderful here. I feel so different now,' she said quietly.

Cal lifted his hand and moved her hair aside as it blew into his face. He dropped a light kiss on her neck, making her shiver.

'Stop talking. You make me feel just too important. I'm not sure what to do with you. Let's see how you make it through the winter. In the meantime, I'll mind how I go.'

'You're not going to drive everyone hard again and work yourself to the bone, are you?'

Cal grinned against her hair. He could just imagine how the boys would take it if he drove them on as he had done these last two weeks. He'd be short-handed when the snow came.

'Oh, I'll have to,' he said in a solemn voice. He couldn't keep it up when she spun round and looked at him in astonishment. He dissolved into laughter. 'Just keep looking the way the horse is going, honey,' he advised. 'That way, we'll both stay in the saddle.'

Laura frowned. 'Stop teasing me.'

'It's not what I want to do but it's all I can do. We could stop and kiss each other speechless but there's no knowing where that would end.'

Laura was silent and when they got back Cal dropped her off at the house and took both horses into the yard.

'Where's Laura?' Tony was there at once when he heard the horses and Cal decided that nonchalance was the best way to deal with the situation.

'I dropped her off at the house. No point in her walking back up there.' He began to unsaddle but Tony still watched him anxiously.

'Did she manage?'

'Sure,' Cal said. 'We went a long way for her first ride.'

'You were a long time. I was worried,' Tony persisted.

'I dropped her off at the house, not into a river,' Cal snapped as his temper rose. 'You should be concentrating on your work instead of your sister.'

Tony turned to go to the barn. He looked mixed up. He didn't seem to be able to decide whether to be annoyed or embarrassed and Mike gave Cal a forbidding frown.

'Don't take your frustration out on the paid help,' he muttered. 'Everything you're getting you're asking for.'

The two friends glared at each other for a moment and then Cal grinned ruefully. 'Know me better than I know myself, don't you?'

'More or less. Mend a few fences while you've got the chance.'

Cal looked across to see Tony just about to disappear

into the stables. 'Come up to the house for dinner, Tiger,' he shouted. 'You and Laura can sit and compare aches and pains.'

Tony grinned, obviously pleased, and Mike took the horses from Cal.

'Told you so,' he murmured. 'That Tiger never stops talking about his sister. Try to separate them and you'll end up losing them both.'

Cal scowled at him. 'I didn't think of trying,' he snapped.

'Thought you could do it with no effort?'

'Listen, you ornery—'

'Yeah.' Mike just led the horses away and when he got to the barn he turned and grinned at Cal. Cal's annoyance drifted away as he grinned back.

Mike knew him all right. They'd come a long way since the days when they would roll in the dust pummelling each other like lunatics. Mike was the closest thing he had to a brother. He'd been sixteen when Josh had brought a resentful and watchful Michael Silver home.

He suddenly felt grateful to his father and his eyes turned to the ranch house. There was something that Laura and Tony ought to see. He set off to show her before he forgot that, sometimes, Josh had made him happy. Charlie too, for that matter.

Laura was soaking in the bath and, when he'd told Biddy there would be one more for dinner, Cal went upstairs to his father's room. The photographs were still where Josh had left them and, for a few moments, Cal wandered around looking at them and at the room his father had used very infrequently over the last few years.

When he thought she would be ready, Cal knocked on Laura's door.

'Come in.' When she called he put his head round the

door. She was still in her dressing gown but neither of them were embarrassed.

Cal held out his hand. 'There's something I want to show you.'

She just came, her bare feet showing below the hem of the robe, and Cal felt another stab of guilt. She looked like a young girl. She had the trust of one too and he vowed to take care of her.

'I want to show you my father's room. I've never had anything moved since he died. I expect I'll have to get around to it but I suppose I've simply put off doing it. I want to show you exactly what meant so much to him.'

She kept her hand in his and he led her along the passage to the last room. It was a very masculine room with dark covers on the bed and old, polished furniture, but the first thing she saw was an enlarged photograph of a woman. It was hanging on the wall facing the bed and she knew who it was without asking.

This would have been the first thing Josh Wexford had seen when he got up in the morning, the last thing he had seen at night—his wife, Cal's mother. She was like Cal with the black hair and blue eyes. She was beautiful and Laura understood why Josh Wexford had lost interest in things when she'd died.

'My mother,' Cal said when Laura stood looking at the photograph. 'He loved her to the exclusion of anything else. When she died I think he would have died too if he hadn't had me to coach to take this ranch over.'

Laura's hand tightened in his and he led her to the big shining chest of drawers. 'This is how he was,' he said softly. 'This is mostly how I remember him.'

There was a photograph of a big smiling man with his arm flung round another man who was also smiling. There was no mistaking Josh Wexford. Tall and strong-looking like Cal, he also had dark hair. The man beside him was good-looking and full of fun, by the look of it. He had a shock of light brown hair and tawny eyes.

'That was your father,' Cal told her. 'That's Charlie, the best friend my father ever had. Without Charlie, I'm sure Josh would have simply died years ago. Tony said he'd never seen his father and you must have few memories. I want you to have this photograph. Maybe it will add to the memories and maybe it will make Tony less bitter.'

Laura turned to him and smiled. 'I was bitter too. Now the bitterness is going because I'm sure my father would have been very unhappy if he'd come home. It was a struggle without a father but it would have been a struggle with him. Some people should never marry and my father was one of those people.'

Cal nodded. 'He was a drifter and a dreamer but he finally settled where he could do most good. I suppose my father should never have married either, because he couldn't live without my mother. Charlie gave him the will to struggle on.'

He put the framed photograph in her hands and she hugged it close. 'Tony's coming for dinner tonight. You can sit by yourselves and look at the photograph. You can also compare bruises.'

Laura grimaced. 'He never complained of feeling like I do. I'll never get to be riding like a cow-hand.'

'Yes, you will,' Cal laughed. 'You'll have to. When you've finished in the office you're going to be taking stock of things round the ranch. I mean to put you to good use.'

Laura turned to the door with a deep sigh. 'By the time I go home, I'll have forgotten how to work in a big office.'

Cal walked beside her and shot her a quick, suspicious glance. 'Did you send that resignation in to your job in England?'

'Not yet.'

'Then hop to it.'

'I haven't really got an excuse.'

Cal put his arm round her and dropped it quickly when he was instantly aware of the silky feel of her. He wondered if she was wearing anything under that robe and his blood began to sizzle again. She was so trusting that he didn't know whether he was a shining knight or a wolf.

'Sure you have,' he said gruffly. 'You've been kid-napped.'

During the next few weeks, Laura learned to ride. Cal had produced a hat, not white like his, but black and a comfortable fit. When she showed surprise he told her that Biddy had got it in town when she went to the shops.

'It will keep the sun off your face and the rain if you get caught out in it.' He looked her over carefully and then nodded. 'It suits you too.'

Now, Laura might not feel like one of the hands, but she rode and she could get out of the saddle at the end of a ride and not feel stiff all over. When Cal was not available, Mike took over the job and she learned to like the silent man who knew horses with an uncanny skill that intrigued her.

When she rode with Cal he was watchful and business-like, never again achingly passionate as he had been on their first ride out. In fact Laura sometimes asked herself if she had imagined all that. He was kind and quiet, he told her more about the ranch and told her tales of her father when she asked.

Tony was invited to eat with them much more and he was changing too. He was much more easygoing and he was much more of a man. He was a man in so many ways that Laura could not deny it. Her brother was flying free and she struggled not to feel frighteningly alone.

Cal noticed as he noticed everything.

'Tony's changed,' he remarked one day when they were riding across the ranch. 'How do you feel about that?'

'Scared, I suppose, but I feel proud of him too. I'm grateful to you.'

'I don't collect gratitude. He's doing a day's work like everyone else. He looks stronger and healthier so why are you scared?'

'Because one day soon he's going to tell me that he wants to simply stay on here. He's going to just drop the idea of university and become a cowboy. After all, that's what boys dream about.'

'I'm a cowboy,' Cal said tightly.

'No, you're not. You're a rich rancher and that's the difference.' She swept her hand around. 'All this belongs to you. It's been in your family for generations. Tony will never have this sort of life because we've got nothing to fall back on except our brains. He needs his education.'

Cal was silent and then he said, 'You're right, of course. Will it help if I make him realise that he's finally got to go back to university, that this is just a job he's doing for his year off?'

'At the moment he'd probably take it better from you. He may not even be thinking about staying, but I have the nasty feeling that he is.'

'I'll speak to him.' Cal shot a quick look at her. 'Now can you settle down and be happy?'

'I am happy,' Laura said, not meeting his eyes. 'Who wouldn't be here?'

Cal didn't answer and Laura knew that in a way she was lying. She should be happy but there was an empty feeling inside her all the time. She would be going one day, leaving this wonderful place, and she knew she would never forget it.

There was Cal too. He had taken her to the very edge of an exciting world and had stopped there. When he touched her it was accidentally and he dropped his hand away as if he were burned.

She blamed herself. Her inexperience had shown and he had noticed. It gave her a feeling of shame. She was twenty-five but the tight control she had lived in all her life showed clearly. There never had been any nights out with friends. Her mother had seen to that. She'd always been needed at home and had never rebelled in case Tony had become involved in an argument.

She didn't know Cal was watching her until he said, 'Let's go back now.'

He was probably tired of her silently thinking, looking gloomy, and Laura wheeled her horse around with easy skill to start the trip back to the ranch.

'You're getting better by the day.'

Cal's praise startled her. She did things now without thought because she expected the horse to obey and she wasn't afraid to ride. In any case, Sky was a gentle creature.

Laura leaned forward and patted the smooth neck. 'It's Sky. I never feel frightened now because I'm sure I can leave it to her.'

'I wouldn't have put you on a horse who wasn't trustworthy. In any case, all the horses on the ranch are working horses. Sky is just lucky. Nobody is allowed to ride her now except you. Mike would have their scalps.'

'So I should ride her every day?' Laura asked, looking at him with surprise. 'I didn't know she was set aside for me.'

'Sky is yours. Mike gives her exercise when you're not available, but that's all.'

'Do you ride her?'

'I never have the time. Mike makes time. He can tell by the look in their eyes when a horse needs something. Sometimes Sky needs a good gallop. When you're ready to do that, then she's your complete responsibility.'

'I can gallop now,' Laura stated, and before he could order her not to she set off with a determination that took him by surprise. She was riding fast, Sky instantly dropping into an easy rhythm.

Cal was beside her in a second and he was angry, more angry than she'd ever seen him. He reached over and pulled her out of the saddle as he ordered Sky to stop. Then he turned blazing eyes on Laura.

'Don't you ever do that again!' He rapped out the words at her and she sat perfectly still in front of him. She was too startled to answer and when he lowered her to the ground she stood looking up at him in horror.

'Stop looking like that!' He swung out of the saddle and grabbed her arms. 'I'm not about to kill you. Do anything so foolish again and you'll be likely to kill yourself.'

'I—I was perfectly safe,' Laura stammered.

'How the hell do you know? If Sky had stumbled when you were going at that speed, you haven't the skill to keep in the saddle.'

'I can ride now.'

'You're *learning* to ride now! You're weeks from galloping and then not as fast as that.'

'Tony galloped the first time he got into the saddle and you never shouted at him.'

'He galloped slowly round the yard and I'm not shouting!'

'Roaring, then. Call it what you will, you're being nasty and I don't have to put up with it.'

'You'll put up with anything I say while you're on the Bar W!'

'Then I'll get off the Bar W!'

She turned to walk away, not caring where she was, and Cal grabbed her, sweeping her into his arms before she could take more than a step.

'God, Laura. Promise me you'll not do anything like that again.' He buried his face in her hair and held her tight. 'You're not Tony. You're fragile whether you want to be or not. I don't want to see you lying on the grass all broken and hurt. I couldn't bear it.'

He drew back to look at her and his face was pale. 'My mother died like that and she could ride like a ranch hand. Accidents happen. No accident is going to happen to you.'

'I'm so sorry, Cal. I didn't know.' Laura reached up and touched his face gently. 'I promise I'll not go riding again.'

'I don't want that sort of promise. I don't want to stop you having fun. I know you like this horse and I know you want to ride. All I'm asking is that you take care. A little at a time, Laura.'

He stood looking down at her, staring into her eyes, and Laura managed a tremulous smile.

'You don't have to will me to obey. I'll not do it again. I promised.'

'I'm not willing you to obey,' he said thickly. 'I'm willing myself not to kiss you.'

'Why?' She looked so wistful that he held her close again.

'Because...because you're so different. You're more than I can handle. I thought I could handle anything but I can't seem to manage it with you.'

'I don't know what I'm doing wrong.' Laura's eyes filled with tears and he bent his dark head and sought her lips in a wild way that stopped her breath.

'Oh, Laura, Laura,' he whispered when the breathtaking kiss was over. 'You're not doing anything wrong. It's me. I'm trying so damned hard not to do anything wrong that it's likely to kill me. I've never been a guardian before and I'm still learning the rules. Have patience with me, will you?'

Laura put her arms round his waist and her head on his shoulder. 'I don't need a guardian.'

'Oh, yes, you do. You're getting one whether you like it or not. I'll get the hang of it sooner or later, even if I have to ask Mike to beat me up like he used to.'

He swung her up into her own saddle before he was tempted further and Laura looked down at him with outrage in her dark eyes.

'Mike used to beat you up?'

'We used to beat each other up when we were teenagers.'

He mounted and grinned across at her. 'I told you we grew up here together. Mike was fourteen, raw and mean as a polecat when he came to the Bar W. He'd been getting into trouble with the law when Dad rescued him. I was mean because I'd just lost my mother and I resented Dad bringing Mike onto the place. We settled our differences with our fists. Frank bathed our cuts and kept a wary eye on us.'

'What about your father? Didn't he try and stop you?'

'No,' Cal said with a reminiscent smile. 'He knew we both needed to take our grudges and our grief out on someone. When we finally got round to stopping, we were friends. We've been friends ever since.'

Laura was silent. She had never lived life so fully, never felt the need to fight for supremacy because there was no way she could ever have it. Her father hadn't been there and her mother had had all the supremacy. Laura had just had responsibilities and duty. There had never been this free, wild life and she knew she had missed something that would never come now.

'What are you thinking?' Cal asked.

'I'm thinking that you've lived a good life. You've been free, in spite of any grief. I feel as if I've never been free in my life. Maybe that makes me a bad daughter, but that's how I feel.'

'According to Tony you were a very good daughter.'

'He certainly seems to talk about me a lot,' Laura said impatiently. 'Some things I prefer to keep to myself.'

'Then why did you tell me?'

'I don't know,' Laura said with a frown. 'You have a way of making me confess all the time. It's probably because you're my self-appointed guardian.'

'That's probably it,' Cal said wryly. 'Seems I'm getting the hang of this guardian business after all.'

He was silent from then on, wondering if they would both have been better served if Charlie had kept his children with him. They would have had all the freedom they'd wanted then, and more besides.

He glanced at Laura and changed his mind. She wouldn't have had that look about her. She wouldn't have been a mixture of sweetness and temper. Charlie would not have settled here and given a new lease of life to Josh either.

'Things work out for the best,' Laura said quietly, almost echoing his thoughts.

'They sure enough do,' Cal muttered. He looked up at the sky. 'We'll get an early fall of snow soon. The wind's colder and the clouds are heavy over the Rockies. You'll need some warmer clothes. We'll go along to town in the morning and get you and Tony fitted out.'

Laura turned round in the saddle. Her eyes were startled and embarrassed. 'You can't do that. We can go and fit ourselves out.'

'No, you can't,' Cal said stubbornly. 'You both work for me.'

'You know perfectly well that I'll not countenance such a thing. I'll pay for our things.'

'And spend the money you've earned? It's supposed to be for setting you up in England.'

'All the same,' Laura snapped. 'I'll pay our bills.'

'What's the problem?' Cal asked sarcastically. 'You afraid somebody will think you're a kept woman?'

'I will be if I let you pay for my things,' Laura glared at him. 'You—you just say anything that comes into your head without any thought of the consequences to Tony and me.'

'Before you say something unforgivable, you'd better stop and think. Unless you intend to be cooped up in the house for the winter you need the sort of clothes we find necessary here. They don't come cheap. Tony will be working outdoors in any case. He works for me. *You* work for me. I buy your outfits for the winter.'

Laura just scowled at him and rode off. He started to follow but slowed down when he noticed the ranch buildings coming up. She wasn't going fast and probably wouldn't come to any harm. All the same, he was anxious until he saw her dismounting in the yard.

And he was doing some scowling himself. He could handle a mad steer more easily than he could handle Laura. He felt he was stepping onto new ground for the first time in his life. Why couldn't she be simple? Why did she have to go from soft, dreamy enchantment to prickly irritation without pause?

By the time he rode in, she'd disappeared and Mike came out to greet him.

'There'll be snow on the way soon.'

'I know,' Cal snapped, unsaddling and looking tight-lipped.

'Trouble?' Mike asked innocently and Cal spun round and snarled at him.

'Can you remember the time when I haven't had trouble?' He hefted the saddle and set off for the stables. 'It's Laura,' he said more quietly. 'I've never met a woman like her.'

'No, you haven't,' Mike murmured, bringing Cal's horse along. 'Go easy. She's not sure where she fits as yet.'

'She fits here,' Cal snapped.

'She fits here because Tony's here. Time will come when he goes back to that university. She'll have no need to fit here then.'

The thought of it kept Cal silent and Mike watched him with all-knowing black eyes. 'Thought I'd mention it,' he said.

'Yeah. You mentioned it,' Cal growled.

It needed mentioning because sometimes he forgot. Obviously, Laura did not forget. She'd already pointed out the difference between them, that he was rich, the owner of all this land, while she and Tony needed their wits to survive. She was terrified he would offer charity and prickly as a porcupine when she suspected it.

He was used to things being straightforward. If something was needed he did it. If someone wanted something he gave it. It was a code he lived by. Why couldn't Laura accept that?

By the time he got up to the house he had worked himself into a rage, partly from frustration and partly from feeling helpless in the face of her stubbornness.

Laura wasn't anywhere to be seen. He stood at the foot of the stairs and roared for her. She had accused him of roaring so she might as well be at the receiving end of it.

'What is it?' She came to the top of the stairs and looked down at him. She had changed already and that meant she had gone straight up to her room, doubtless to brood about things.

'Come into my office. I want to speak to you,' he said abruptly. He then walked off and Laura came slowly downstairs. He was angry and she knew it must be about her. She wasn't looking forward to this interview, because that was what it was to be. But she was adamant that she would pay for their winter clothes, no matter how enraged he became.

When she walked into Cal's office he was sitting at the desk and he glared at her. 'Close the door,' he ordered. 'I can do without Biddy hearing everything.'

'I expect she heard you roaring at the bottom of the stairs,' Laura muttered as she closed the door. 'They probably heard you in the yard.'

He was on his feet in an instant, rounding the desk and coming towards her with long strides. To his astonishment, she backed away.

'If you think you can frighten me into submission, then you're mistaken,' she said with a scared look of defiance. 'I make my own mind up about things and no amount of intimidation will alter that.'

It stopped him in his tracks and cooled his temper like a drenching in cold water. 'Intimidate you? You think I'd do that? Where have you got the idea that I'm an uncivilized bully?'

'I—I haven't, but you were coming at me fast as if you meant to subdue me.'

'Oh, thank you, Laura,' he said bitterly, turning away from her. 'You've just given me the perfect end to a lousy day. First you try to kill yourself right in front of my eyes, then you pick a fight about a few goddamn clothes. Now

I'm a bully, a brute who's hell-bent on scaring you. No wonder you're so edgy about staying on at the ranch.'

'I—I'm not,' Laura stammered.

'You could have fooled me and about fifty other guys.' He turned his head and scowled at her. His eyes were narrowed and piercing. 'Everything you say is a mountain-sized hint that you'll soon be long gone.'

He turned away again and stared angrily out of the window at the gathering night and Laura's defiance suddenly crumbled. Tears of regret, sadness and longing filled her eyes and spilled onto her flushed cheeks. She cried absolutely silently, her fair head bent and her shoulders shaking.

Cal turned after a while and his face was stunned when he saw her crying so deeply and so quietly. He was beside her before she even knew it and he folded her close, his hand enclosing the silky shine of her hair.

'Don't cry, Laura,' he begged thickly. 'Don't cry, honey. I have no excuse for roaring at you.'

'I—I've got no excuse for giving you a bad day,' she wept. 'It—it's just that I don't always understand you. You're so different from me and I'm afraid of doing something wrong.'

He perched on the edge of his desk and pulled her closer. 'You never do one single thing wrong,' he murmured. 'I'm the one with all the wrongdoing piling up against me.'

'Oh, no.' Laura lifted tear-drenched eyes and looked shocked. 'You never do anything wrong. You've been so good to us that it's hard to believe.'

'Why is it so hard to believe? You know you're needed round here. You know I can't cope with all my office papers. I never meant to be charitable, if that's what you're afraid of. But why can't I buy you some winter clothes? Why can't I take care of you? That's something I would do for anyone who came here.'

Laura looked down and when he pulled her closer she buried her face against his shoulder. It was so comfortable that she had to stifle the sigh that sprang to her lips. To be wrapped in his hard warm arms was as much like heaven as she could imagine.

'It's not the same, is it?'

'Why isn't it?' He tilted her face and looked at her solemnly. 'Because I want you?'

When she looked up at him with questioning eyes he pulled her even closer, parting his legs until she was pressed against his body. He took a deep steadying breath when she came so willingly.

'Is that what you're really fighting about? You're fighting because you know I want you?'

'I—I don't know.'

'Isn't it glaringly obvious?' He held her against him, looking into her eyes until they closed slowly. He was hard and aroused, his hands were slowly caressing her, moving over her back with warm, questing strokes that made her feel as if she were melting. When she didn't answer he bent his head and found her lips and she instantly surrendered.

He teased her lips open and his searching tongue moved into the warm darkness of her mouth. His hands tightened on her when she gasped and moved further into him.

'I can't go on avoiding you,' he whispered against her lips. 'It's killing me.'

He had no chance to say anything else because Laura wrapped her arms around his neck and gave way to all the longing that had been building up since the day she had first seen him. When his lips found hers again she kissed him back with an urgency that took his breath away.

Within seconds they were locked in a heated embrace, tongues questing, their lips draining each other, and Cal's hands found her surging breasts, stroking the hard nipples with urgent, burning fingers.

Laura gave an excited cry and pressed further against him, her body begging for more until finally he had to pull away from her. She was trembling and he was breathing hard and fast.

'Laura, sweetheart,' he said raggedly. 'This has got to stop right here or it's got to go on until I can't stop.' He buried his face against her neck, breathing in the perfume of her skin. 'Now do you know I want you? Do you know why I want to do everything for you, why I need to keep you here?'

'Yes.' She nodded solemnly, looking up at him with dark-eyed wonder.

'Then let me,' he whispered. 'Let me look after you. Let me buy you things, care for you, make you happy.'

She nodded, too overwhelmed to speak, and just at that moment Biddy knocked on the door.

'Dinner in five minutes,' she called and Cal found it possible to smile.

'We came very close to being the talk of the Bar W just then.'

Laura's face flooded with colour and he took pity on her.

'You've got five minutes to freshen up and I've got five minutes to get changed,' he said, turning her to the door. 'Tony is coming for dinner tonight and if he suspects anything then I'll have no alternative but to beat him up.'

CHAPTER SIX

NEXT day it was colder. A sharp wind blew from the mountains and Cal pointed this out at breakfast time.

'The first stirring of winter. Tomorrow it will probably be warm again but we don't ignore sudden changes in temperature. Today we'll go down into Leviston. I've already told Tiger. We'll leave as soon as we've eaten and I hope you're not about to make a fuss.'

Laura shrugged. 'I'm not fussing. I could do with a trip out anyway.' She looked very interested. 'What do you do with the cattle when it snows? Do you bring them all in to the ranch?'

Cal threw his head back and laughed. 'Honey, we just don't have a barn big enough to bed down five thousand head of cattle.'

'They'll be cold when it snows.'

'They're used to it. If we find any new calves before the snow hits, we'll bring them in, but the rest of the herd take their chances. We fly out and drop feed and see to any that look as if they need us.'

'You fly?'

'We've got a helicopter. Mike and I usually go out and look around. But before the snow comes we all have to search the high ground for strays and bring them down. I think Tiger is just about ready to join us when we go up into the hills.'

He was watching her intently but she didn't ask if Tony would be in any danger. She was learning but he didn't know how long this state of affairs would last.

When Tony came up to the house it was time to go into Leviston and Cal hoped that last night had made her see reason about winter gear. He didn't want another outburst.

They took the Explorer and this time Laura was not asleep. She was able to look around and see what beautiful country she'd missed on the way to the Bar W. The road was good into town and they were soon turning into the one and only street.

As Cal parked they were hailed by a big man who sauntered across to them. Cal introduced him as Ben Chalmers.

'Heard about you two,' Chalmers said. 'You look like Charlie,' he added, nodding to Tony. 'You're much more beautiful than Charlie was, ma'am.'

He was smiling at Laura and Cal nudged Tony. 'Don't take any notice, Tiger. Ben opens that big mouth of his and thinks later. You're not all that ugly.'

They were all grinning and Laura realised that Tony fitted into this atmosphere as if he'd been born to it. She was the one who felt edgy and unsure. She didn't know what she was to Cal. She didn't know exactly what he meant when he said he wanted her.

Of course the expression itself said everything, but Cal didn't seem the sort of man who would indulge in mindless sex. He was gentle and kind to her and his attitude left her hopelessly lost.

Cal tucked her hand under his arm and prepared to move off. The conversation had become completely cattle orientated as soon as the weather had been mentioned and even Tony was looking at the sky with a certain amount of expertise.

'Can't hang around second-guessing the weather,' Cal said. 'We're in town to shop—even if it kills us,' he added under his breath, with a wry glance at Laura.

Ben Chalmers gave Laura a fatherly smile, slapped Tony

on the back with enough enthusiasm to almost knock him off his feet, and they went on their way to the few shops. Cal looked very cautious about the whole expedition but Laura was suddenly happy.

For the first time since she had been a child, someone was looking after her, making sure she had warm clothes for the winter. Cal was actually bringing her to the shops with a certain grim determination.

She gave a little chuckle and Cal looked at her uneasily. 'Is that giggling?'

'Probably.' She smiled up at him. 'I was just thinking you've managed to get the hang of this guardian business.'

He tightened her to his side. 'Like hell I have. I'm just good at bluffing my way out of trouble. Don't bank on it lasting.'

'Don't bank on what lasting?' Tony came up to them after stopping to gaze with longing at a shop with hunting rifles in the window.

'The easy weather,' Cal said smoothly. 'I reckon it's time you had some real boots, Tiger.'

'Like yours?' Tony cast a look of admiration at Cal's boots.

'Yeah, like mine.' He looked down at Laura. 'You want some cowboy boots, Laura? You being a real rider now, you should have the gear.'

'I should spend as little as possible,' Laura pointed out with a worried look back on her face.

'If you're going to be awkward, I aim to roar at you. Behave yourself. Remember that any scene will be the talk of the town for years to come. In fact, if they don't mention it, I'll bring it up myself.'

There was no scene because when Laura got inside the shop and saw the array of winter jackets and trousers she was like a child in a sweet shop. She was even persuaded to get some long johns, and when they were about to leave with their purchases Cal simply said, 'Put this on the Bar W account.'

He waited until Tony was packing the car and then bent to whisper in Laura's ear, 'Didn't hurt at all, did it?'

'Not much.' She gave a low gurgling laugh that drew Cal's eyes to her lips.

'When we get back, you can teach me how to giggle like that,' he said. 'We'll call it even then.' His eyes roamed over her flushed face before he turned her to the car. 'If we stand around here much longer I'm going to start kissing you and I've got to learn that I can't have everything my eye falls on.'

'I thought you always got your own way?' Laura asked daringly.

'Don't push your luck,' he said, sliding into the driving seat. 'This sort of teasing can bring its own retribution.'

'I didn't mean to tease you,' Laura said quickly.

'Tease away. I'm game.'

'Game for what?' Tony climbed into the Explorer at the tail-end of the conversation.

'For just about anything,' Cal said, casting an amused glance at Laura's flushed face. 'You ready to round up a few steers tomorrow, Tiger?'

'Can I?'

'I sure hope so. Give you the chance to try out your new boots.' Cal glanced across at Laura. 'Want to come with us?'

'Oh, can I?' She looked as happy as a child and Cal grinned at her.

'If you're very, very good,' he promised.

When they got back and had lunch, Cal went out to join the men and Laura began to put her new clothes away. She sang to herself as she moved around the bedroom and when she caught sight of her reflection in the mirror she was smiling. She had never been so happy before in her whole life.

She knew what had kept her father here and there was no bitterness in her now. Responsibilities had been lifted from her shoulders as though they had never been. They had been lifted by a quietly determined man who simply took on the burdens himself.

Laura had stopped looking for motives. Cal even controlled his desire for her. He was content to see everyone happy and though she knew he had a frightening temper it rarely showed.

Her happy thoughts were interrupted by a crash on the stairs and the sound of Biddy's voice as she cried out in pain. Laura rushed out of her room and saw Biddy at the bottom of the stairs and it was quite clear what had happened. Biddy had fallen down the stairs and was obviously in agony.

When Laura ran down to her she could see that Biddy's leg was bent at a strange angle and she didn't stop to see what she could do.

'I'll get help,' she shouted as she went flying to the door. 'I'll be back straight away, Biddy. Just hold on for a minute.'

She saw Biddy nod painfully, perspiration rolling down her face, and then Laura erupted out of the door and scanned the yard for help. There were a few men just mounting to go out and Cal was one of them. Laura called but it was obvious they didn't hear her. Soon they would be away from the ranch and there would be no help available.

She raced round to the Explorer, thankful when she found the keys inside, and, starting the engine, Laura spun the heavy vehicle round and set off to stop them. Her hand

was on the horn from the moment she set off and that
gained their attention. By the time she made it down to the
yard and skidded to a halt, they were all out of their saddles
and running towards her.

'What's happened?' Cal was closest as she jumped out
of the car and she yelled at him before he'd covered the
distance.

'Biddy's fallen downstairs. She's broken her leg but I
don't know what else is hurt. Get in, I'll drive you back to
the house.'

Cal got into the passenger seat while Frank got into the
back with Mike as Laura turned the Explorer and headed
back up to the house.

Frank looked terrified. 'It's the boots,' he said. 'She
never will take off those damned boots. And she moves
like a lightning streak, never does anything at a normal
pace.'

He sounded panicky to Laura and she tried to stop his
anxiety.

'She's all right, Frank. She's just in a lot of pain. I don't
think she fell more than a couple of steps. I heard her fall.
She'll feel a lot better when she sees you.'

'I'll cut them boots up.'

'I wouldn't if I were you,' Laura warned, swinging to a
stop at the house. 'One shock a day is more than enough.'

Cal looked at her in surprise as they all piled out of the
car and went into the house. Cal went straight to the phone
as Frank dropped to his knees by Biddy.

'Where do you hurt, darlin'? I've told you about those
damned boots a hundred times.'

'They're comfortable,' Biddy gasped, holding onto him.
'You leave them be.'

'They'll have to be cut off at hospital,' Mike said,

crouching down beside her. 'Better not set too much store by them, Biddy.'

'Just you ease them off, Mike,' Biddy pleaded. 'I've had these boots for years and they're well panned in.'

'No,' Mike said, giving his gentle smile. 'That's a bad break you've got there. That left boot has got to be slit open and cut away.'

'You don't know. You'd only know if I was a horse.' She turned to Frank who was holding her tightly. 'If you still love me, give me a painkiller.'

Laura crouched down beside them. 'Better not, Biddy. They'll want to give you an anaesthetic to set your leg. If you take anything now, they'll probably have to wait and you'll be in even more pain. Stick it out.'

Biddy nodded. 'Okay. Just you ease my boots off then, Laura.'

'I'm not going to do that, Biddy. The pain would be agonising.'

'Not as agonising as losing these boots,' Biddy insisted.

'Ambulance is on its way,' Cal said, coming to join the circle around Biddy. 'I'll buy you some more boots when you get on your feet again.'

'They'll not be like these,' Biddy grumbled.

'I got some new boots this morning,' Laura said to cheer her up. 'They're lovely.'

'They're not panned in. These are panned in.'

'Will you let it go, woman?' Frank muttered. 'We'll be glad to see the back of you when that ambulance comes.'

He leaned forward and gave her a big juicy kiss and Biddy whispered, 'I hurt real bad, Frank.'

'I know, honey. Just you go on about the boots if it helps. We can take it.'

When the ambulance came and Biddy had gone off to

hospital with Frank sitting in the back to hold her hand, Mike turned admiring eyes on Laura.

'You did really well there,' he said. 'Nobody would think you were a town girl.'

'She's full of hidden talents,' Cal muttered. He glanced at Laura. 'Looks like we're eating in the cookhouse for the time being.'

Laura shrugged. 'We can if you like but I told you before—I can cook.'

'So what do you want to do? We can eat with the boys or we can have a scene of quiet domesticity.'

'I'll go and see what we've got,' Laura promised, spinning around and heading for the kitchen. 'I'd rather eat here.'

When Cal looked up, Mike was watching him with dark, calculating eyes.

'Time will come when you've got to make your mind up,' he murmured. 'Seems to me she's starry-eyed about you.'

'She's not like Charlie,' Cal pointed out quietly. 'The pull of home is a strong pull.'

'It's never pulled me,' Mike said with a scowl. 'Home is where the heart is and mine's right here permanently.'

'That's different. You've got a brother here.' Cal opened his hand at the same time that Mike did. There were the same scars that had formed when they'd cut their hands and mixed their blood as teenagers. 'Laura's brother is here for now but he'll go back to England to university. Right now he's happy and excited. It's not going to be excitement all the time, though, and I doubt if he'll want to be here when he's been to university and tasted another life.'

'Only time will tell,' Mike said. 'He'll not forget this place, though, and neither will Laura.'

'Maybe not,' Cal muttered, 'but dreaming about it and living it are two different things.'

'It just depends what the dream is about.'

'Is that an ancient Blackfoot saying?' Cal looked at Mike and grinned.

'Just plain common sense. You coming out or not?'

'I'll see what Laura's doing, then I'll join you. Think the snow will start soon?'

'No. We've got some time yet. Time to get the strays in off the high ground and get everything bedded down.' Mike went to the door and looked up at the sky. 'I'll wait for you in the yard. We'll take Tiger out with us, I reckon he's about ready.'

When Cal walked into the kitchen, Laura was already sorting things out for dinner.

'It may not be as good as Biddy's cooking,' she warned, her eyes on the pans and food she had out onto the tops.

'I'll take my chances if you will.' Cal's eyes were on her when she looked round and he seemed to be very serious.

She looked away nervously. 'Would you rather eat in the cookhouse? Tony says the food is good there.'

'I'd rather eat here. Mike beat me to it when he praised you. You were quick and efficient and you settled Frank better than I could have done without raising my voice.'

'Everybody acts quickly in an emergency.'

'No, they don't. Some people panic. I didn't know you could drive.'

Laura gave a little laugh as she began to prepare vegetables. 'I've been too busy telling you what I can't do to dwell on what I'm good at. I'm gathering skills every day now, though. I can ride—after a fashion, but I still can't swim.'

'We'll get around to that when the snow goes away. It's got to come yet, so swimming will take some time.'

'I know.' Laura nodded and got on with her work. She had hardly looked at him since he'd come into the kitchen.

'Don't be scared of me, Laura,' Cal said quietly. 'We've been alone before and you've never come to any harm.'

'I don't expect to.' She glanced up and as quickly looked away. 'And I'm not scared of you.'

'Then look at me.'

When she obeyed and looked at him, Cal walked slowly towards her. 'You've had an interesting day,' he said, letting his fingers trail down her face. 'It's a pity about Biddy's accident but she'll be all right soon enough. Marge and Helen will come in and do the cleaning as usual. If you want to keep up with the cooking, then go right ahead.'

'But I won't do the ironing,' Laura said quickly. 'I don't like ironing.'

'Then you'll not do it,' Cal said in his soothing voice.

'Don't start patronising me.' Laura scowled at him and got the usual grin.

'Okay, honey.' He dropped a quick kiss on her cheek and walked to the door. 'See you later. If you burn the dinner we can always eat with the boys.' He was gone before Laura could think of a suitable retort and she settled happily in Biddy's kitchen.

With Biddy injured, things seemed to be different. It was true they had the house to themselves in the normal course of events and Laura had never given that a thought. Now, though, she was aware that Cal was alone with her and this brought a tingling excitement that was difficult to control.

Cal got round that with no trouble. He invited Tony to eat with them on a regular basis. Laura wasn't too sure how she felt about that but Cal explained the position to her when he noticed her puzzled looks.

'Everyone knows that Biddy is hurt. It's brought home to them that you and I are alone up here,' he said one day when they were by themselves for a few minutes.

'Has anyone said anything?'

'They have not,' Cal muttered. 'They know better than to tangle themselves in my business. I want you to understand, Laura, that I have to keep your interests in mind. I took over your life when I asked you to stay here. I must admit that I never thought about anything but helping you both. I didn't realise I'd end up wanting you.' He turned away impatiently when she looked at him in what Mike had pointed out was a starry-eyed manner. 'I took on the responsibility,' he bit out. 'I'm not about to take advantage of the situation.'

'You haven't,' Laura pointed out quietly.

He shot a look at her that was a mixture of frustration and amusement. 'I came pretty close to it. Now you're my housekeeper as well as my secretary. I know you trust me, Laura, and, believe me, I'll live up to that trust even if it kills me.'

'Biddy's home already. When she's fit to come in to work again, things will be back to normal.'

Cal laughed and ruffled her hair. 'If I didn't know you better I would think that was an invitation, Miss Hughes.' When her cheeks went a rosy pink he groaned and held her hands tightly. 'Leave it be, Laura. When Tony goes home I know you'll go with him. I'm not about to take advantage of you now and ruin the rest of your life. I'm your guardian. Understand?'

Laura nodded. 'You're my guardian. I understand.'

He gave her a close look and then walked out and Laura felt let down, saddened, as if the spark had gone out of her life. She pulled herself together, though, and counted her blessings. She was piling up her savings, she lived in this lovely place and Cal was good to her.

She had taken a chance on this trip to Canada and he had scooped both Tony and herself up into his life for no other reason but that he was like that. She vowed she would not show in any way how deeply she felt about him.

He kept his word too. Even before Biddy was back at the house the business of rounding up strays had to be tackled and Cal invited her to join the men as they rode into the hills.

By now Laura was a good enough rider to stay with them and Tony was good enough to take his share of the work. He rode with Mike and she felt really proud of him when she saw him bringing cattle to join the steadily growing herd that Cal and Frank controlled. It was really exciting to hear the whistles and high-pitched shouts as the ranch hands drove the strays down out of the trees and brought them to Cal and his foreman.

Frank gave her his rope and showed her how to slap it against the saddle and flick it towards any recalcitrant steer and she loved it all.

'We'll have you as good as a regular cowboy soon, Laura.' He smiled. Since her help with Biddy, Frank had shown a fatherly interest in her, and when Cal grinned across at her Laura felt more at home than she had ever felt in her life. She knew this was only a sort of working holiday but she dreaded going back to England now.

The days were drawing in towards winter and each morning there was a white glaze of frost on the ground and on the grass in the pastures. The sun was still bright and warm and it soon melted any frost but all the signs were there of approaching winter and even Laura had learned to watch the sky for signs of snow.

When Biddy was finally back at work, Laura took every opportunity to get out of the house. She had the office under control now so she rode every day and Mike showed her how to clean saddles and help out in the yard. Like Tony, she looked healthy and sure of herself.

All that security ended when one day a car came into the yard and a very glamorous woman got out.

'Hi, Mike,' she called. 'Where's Cal?'

'Out with the boys,' Mike was not friendly and Laura could hear it in his voice. He had warmed towards her but now his face was hard-looking. His eyes were still as black, the bronzed planes of his face were suddenly very apparent. For some reason Laura knew he was staring at an enemy.

'Point me in the right direction and I'll go and find him. You could saddle a horse for me,' the newcomer said in a rather arrogant voice.

Mike turned without a word and went to saddle up for her. His face showed nothing but Laura could almost feel his anger. This woman was speaking to him as if he were a servant, as if he just worked here and was forced to do her bidding. Laura knew that Mike was much more than that at the Bar W. He was Cal's friend, his brother.

It was her turn then. So far she had been ignored and now the woman turned hard green eyes on her, eyes that made a rapid inventory of her clothes, her hair and her beautiful face.

'The Wexford ranch is taking on women?' she asked scathingly. 'What can you do—wrestle steers?'

Before Laura could answer Mike was there, leading a horse out, and she was surprised at the speed he'd done it.

'Miss Hughes and her brother are staying on the ranch for a year. They're friends of the boss.'

His voice was stony and Laura shot a startled glance at him. He never called Cal the boss. He never called her Miss Hughes either. He was getting to be a friend and she was surprised by his attitude.

'Hughes? You're surely not anything to do with Charlie?'

'He was my father,' Laura said quietly.

'You don't look like him.' The woman swung easily into the saddle and looked down at Laura with some amount of scorn. 'Don't tell me you thought he owned the Bar W.'

'No, I didn't think that. We came to see where he used to live.'

'What a wild thing to do.' The woman set the horse in motion, ignored them both and rode out of the yard when Mike pointed her in the direction Cal had taken.

Both Laura and Mike stood looking after her, thinking their own thoughts. She was an expert horsewoman and there was no mistaking that. She was also glamorous and dressed like a movie star, everything about her sleek and well groomed from her pale-coloured jeans to the expensive shirt she wore.

She obviously knew Cal too and the thought of that brought a feeling of instant misery.

'Who is she?' Laura looked up at Mike but he didn't turn his dark gaze away from the disappearing woman.

'Felicity Rayner. She knows Cal. She used to live in Leviston but she moved to Edmonton last year.'

'She's very glamorous,' Laura said quietly.

'She knows what she wants,' Mike muttered. 'Wish I'd left the cinch loose when I saddled up. She could do with a good fall, preferably into cold water.'

Laura had never heard him speak like that and she would

have laughed, but somehow she didn't feel like laughing. She had seemed to be getting to know everybody but Cal obviously lived a life she knew nothing of. She had been stupid to think otherwise.

'I'd better go and get changed,' she said with a gloomy feeling that her idyllic life here was just about over. 'Thanks for troubling with me, Mike.'

'You're no trouble, Laura. Tiger's no trouble either.' He looked down at her with suddenly warm eyes. 'I'm getting to like the English. Can't think why we ever tried to kill them way back.'

Laura laughed and turned away to go to the house. Mike turned back to the barn, but before she went he said quietly, 'She wants Cal. Always did. Thought I should mention it.'

Laura managed a smile and then went on her way. She was glad he'd mentioned it. Now she would know not to intrude when Felicity Rayner came up to the house because she obviously intended to do just that. Laura was not surprised at the misery the knowledge brought. Now she didn't feel like looking up at the blue sky. Her eyes didn't stray to the mountains. She just walked steadily to the ranch house and didn't look further than her own feet.

Mike watched her from the door of the barn and his face was as coldly impassive as his forebears. Give him weapons, a change of clothes and a feather in his night-black hair and he was like a painting from the past.

Felicity Rayner came in when Cal came back. Laura had warned Biddy that there might very well be another for dinner and had told her who it was. Biddy had said nothing but her looks had been pretty much like Mike's, without the air of danger he had been giving off.

Laura changed for dinner and she was in the study, trying to keep her mind occupied, when Cal came to find her. Felicity Rayner came too and clearly she didn't intend to be left out of things. When Cal opened the study door she was right there with him.

'We've got a visitor for dinner,' Cal said when Laura looked up. 'This is Felicity Rayner. She told me she met you in the yard when she came.'

'We met,' Laura said, struggling to smile. 'Did you have a good ride, Miss Rayner?'

'I always have a good ride. I hear you're just learning to ride and making yourself useful round here.'

'Laura never stops making herself useful,' Cal said. He smiled at Laura. 'Come on. Help me to entertain our guest.'

'I—I'll come when dinner's ready,' Laura said quickly. 'I've got plenty to do here and I don't want to intrude when you have a visitor.'

'Oh, I'm not simply a visitor,' Felicity said with a superior smile. 'I know my way around here. There's no need to look after me, Cal. I'll just pop along and wash up for dinner.'

She disappeared in a way that showed she certainly did know her way about and Cal came further into the room, his eyes piercingly on Laura.

'Come out from behind that desk and tell me what's troubling you,' he ordered softly.

'Nothing is troubling me,' Laura said, trying for a mystified look. She didn't fool Cal at all.

He was suddenly frowning down at her. His eyes were no longer laughing and tolerant. 'I've known Felicity for a long time. I also know her family. When I have to go to Edmonton I visit them. Now Felicity is visiting me. You will come to the table and behave yourself because if you imagine that you're about to sulk in your room with a tray of food, then you can think again.'

'I don't sulk,' Laura said in an outrage. 'With Miss

Rayner patronising and you tolerating me, I'll choke on my food.'

His hand came hard and tight on her chin and he tilted it to stare into her eyes. His own eyes narrowed and then his face softened.

'Why, you're jealous, Laura,' he said quietly. 'You're jealous because another woman is going to be sitting at the table with us. Don't worry. I'd rather be sitting at the kitchen table with you and eating what you cook. That's my idea of dinner, just the two of us warm and cosy.'

Laura pulled away from his hand and turned her face away too. 'Don't be ridiculous. Of course I'm not jealous.'

'Let's see.' With no warning he had her in his arms and his lips were on hers. Laura struggled this time but he held her fast and she couldn't resist any persuasion from Cal. She gave a wistful little moan and wound her slender arms round his neck.

They were back where they had been at once, with Cal's lips draining hers and his hands urging her closer. She opened her mouth when his tongue became insistent and, at the feel of the dark, secret warmth he found, Cal's hand came urgently to her breasts. His fingers found her tight nipples, urging them to life, and she cried out against his mouth, pressing herself against the hard, masculine body with the same urgency he showed.

Dimly she heard Felicity come back across the hall, heard her footsteps pause and then leave, but Laura could not have drawn away if her life had depended on it.

Cal held her tightly as he released her mouth and sank his head against her hair. 'God! I want you,' he whispered against her ear. 'You want me too. If it were any other woman, I'd cancel dinner and take you upstairs. Why do you have to be Charlie's girl? Why didn't I meet you somewhere else?'

'I—I can't help being who I am,' Laura said against his face. She was almost sobbing with feeling, trembling against him, and he held her more gently, willing her to calm down after the devastation of his kisses.

'No, you can't help being who you are, Laura. And I can't help being who I am. You're here and I have to look after you. I just can't seem to stop myself from reaching for you, but I've got to keep you safe.' He lifted his head and began to smooth her hair, but he didn't smile. Instead his eyes searched her face and he looked strained.

'We're back where we started. This is where I go and change and you go to freshen up and pull yourself together. You go first, Laura. I don't trust myself to walk up the stairs with you.'

CHAPTER SEVEN

FELICITY was on her best behaviour when they sat down to dinner. Laura couldn't fault her and even began to think she had mistaken the other woman's attitude. Whatever she had been like before, now she was charming, drawing Laura into the conversation, and gradually Laura relaxed.

Maybe jealousy had made her dislike Felicity before. Maybe Mike's attitude was because they'd had some disagreement she didn't know about.

'What will you be doing tomorrow, Cal?' When Felicity asked this question Laura tightened up again, but she need not have worried.

'We'll be bringing the herd in closer. The boys are setting up a few pole barns behind the main buildings, just in case the weather defeats us, but mainly we're driving the cattle closer. After that we're about ready to face the winter. According to Mike we have time yet and he's not often wrong about the weather.'

'I've got a week before I go back. I'll be along to help in the morning.'

'You'll have to find us unless you're here at five,' Cal pointed out. 'We'll be starting early.'

'I'll find you,' Felicity promised. She turned to Laura. 'Are you going out to round up the herd, Laura?'

'I'd like to, if I won't be in the way,' Laura answered, looking at Cal. He'd avoided her eyes all during the meal but now he couldn't. He glanced across at her.

'If you really want to come, then come. It's a long day in the saddle, though.'

'I've got an idea,' Felicity chirped up quickly. 'Why doesn't Laura come with me? It would cut out the length of time in the saddle.'

'If that's what she wants.' Cal didn't look at Laura again. It annoyed her.

'Shall I meet you here?' She glanced at Felicity and got such a pleasant smile that she was left feeling guilty about her previous thoughts.

'I'll be here at about ten. Are you certain you'll feel up to this?'

'She helped bring the strays down from the high ground,' Cal murmured. 'She managed that all right.'

'Really? You seem to have done quite a lot for a city girl.'

'Laura is a fast learner.' As Cal said this Laura tried to keep the colour from rushing into her face. It was a very careful swipe at her as far as she could see. She'd certainly learned fast with Cal and he knew it. If she hadn't done he wouldn't now be feeling frustrated and guilty.

She hadn't been careful enough with him. Her inexperience had shown all along and she had simply been too ready to fall into his arms. Anyone else would have stepped back and been outraged but she had been all too eager.

Laura disappeared to her room as soon as she could and went on feeling the same. In spite of everything Cal had said she knew deep down that this was all her fault. She was left with the impression that she had thrown herself at him from the first.

Felicity had brought her car up to the house and when Laura heard it pull away she breathed a sigh of relief. No chance now of being asked to go back down and join them as they sat and talked. She got ready for bed with that small worry out of her mind but she was just getting into bed when Cal knocked on the door.

When she answered his knock she expected to be berated for going off and leaving before Felicity went.

Cal chose to ignore that small error. He looked down at her as she stood all demure and quiet in the doorway. Even her hands were folded in front of her and she was wearing the same silky robe she had worn before.

Cal's mouth tightened to one harsh line. 'I wanted to ask you if you really are thinking of going out to help with the cattle tomorrow?'

'Not if you think I'll be in the way.'

He gave a slight frown. 'You'll not be in the way. We're not planning to have a stampede. If I'm too involved I can guarantee that Mike will be keeping an eye on you. He seems to have taken you under his wing just like he took to Tony. Very fatherly is Mike, for one so young.'

'He's very nice to me,' Laura said quietly, feeling hurt. 'He's helping me and there's no need to be sarcastic about it.'

'Oh, I know all that. If there's anyone I *do* know, it's Mike. I count him as my brother and I'm not being sarcastic either. I'm being bloody-minded.'

'Well, keep it to yourself,' Laura snapped. 'I'm just the hired help around here. Nobody was bloody-minded to me in my last employment.'

Cal's eyebrows shot up in surprise, then he looked annoyed.

'Listen, you little wildcat—'

'And another thing,' Laura interrupted, 'there was no need to say I'm a fast learner. *You're* the one who's teaching me.'

For a second, Cal looked positively murderous, but Laura stood up to him. She was feeling guilty and hurt and lots of other things but she refused to back down. He watched her for another second and then just turned and walked off to his own room.

Laura was instantly distressed. She ran out into the passage and called to him.

'Cal. I'm sorry. I'm sorry.'

He turned to look at her and then pointed one brown finger at her door.

'Get back inside that room and close the door,' he snapped. 'The way I feel right at this moment, that room is just about the only place where you're safe.'

He was standing with his hands clenched and Laura knew it was useless to argue with him tonight. She knew he was not forgiving either, and she turned and trailed back to her room while Cal watched her with blue-eyed fury.

When she closed her door he went into his room and Laura knew he'd got there because he slammed the door in a rage.

When Laura caught a glimpse of herself in the mirror she was white as a sheet. She knew why he was so angry. She had been as pointedly nasty as she could be. She had chosen to forget all the things he had done for her and had picked on that one little remark about her being a fast learner.

Now she wasn't even too sure it had been a careful swipe at her. She had been trying to learn everything about the ranch. In her own way she was as eager as Tony and Cal had been kind and indulgent. It was just her temper and her jealousy. She readily admitted that and now Cal would be furious for the rest of her time here.

Laura got into bed and put her head under the clothes with frantic thoughts of dying in the night from lack of breath. That thought was soon vanquished when she considered his words. He had said she was only safe in her room. Perhaps he hadn't meant to kill her after all. She was sorry she'd retreated because she knew she was all too ready to bring everything he wanted down on her head.

Laura didn't hear Cal leave next morning. When she got up the yard was almost deserted. She'd slept well but the funny feelings were still there inside her. She wondered if Cal had glared at her door this morning as he'd gone past, and she hurried to get ready as the wonderful thought slid into her mind that perhaps he'd given some thought to waking her.

By the time Felicity came, Laura had her horse saddled and was ready. She was talking to one of the older ranch hands as Felicity drove into the yard. This morning Felicity's face was wreathed in smiles, she even saddled her own horse, and Laura was thankful not to have to countenance more bad tempers. Facing Cal was going to be hard enough after last night's outburst.

'That's a nice little mare you've got there,' Felicity remarked as they rode out.

Laura patted Sky's neck and smiled. 'She's a beauty. Cal gave her to me while I'm here. She's very calm. Just what I need.'

'So you're staying a year as Mike said?'

'I hope so. Cal had a lot of work for me in his office but I've got control of that now. I'm hoping to teach him how to use his computer but he's not too willing to try. He insists that I'll be doing everything. How he'll manage when I've gone I don't know. I expect he'll get into a muddle again with those papers.'

'He's been managing without you for years. I expect he'll manage when you're gone.' Felicity sounded a bit hard and Laura looked at her in surprise. They were out of sight of the ranch now and riding along towards the herd but so far she couldn't see any sign of other riders.

She decided to watch her tongue in future. After all it was her tongue that had got her into trouble last night.

'I imagine he will,' she said quietly.

'I heard about you and your brother in town,' Felicity said after a while. 'Apparently you just came out of the blue and dropped yourselves on Cal.'

Laura began to feel annoyed. 'We didn't drop ourselves on Cal at all. When he met us he just scooped us up and took us to the ranch. We were supposed to stay there for one night but the next day he offered us jobs.'

'Why should he? After all, you're nothing to Cal.'

'Tony will be going back to England to university next year. He wanted to learn about the ranch and Cal offered him a job while he's here. He wanted me to help with his paperwork so it suited us nicely.'

'Well, Cal has always been good-natured,' Felicity said with a reminiscent smile. 'I should know. We were going out together when I lived in Leviston. I went to Edmonton because my parents wanted to go but I wish I hadn't. Cal was angry about it but it was the best thing at the time. Now I'm ready to come back and take up where we left off.'

Laura's heart sank to her feet but she managed to keep her face indifferent.

'We'll probably be gone before then,' she murmured.

She had a dreadful picture in her mind of Felicity seeing her in Cal's arms last night. She knew now exactly who she was—someone who was available and more than ready to be captured.

Felicity gave a sudden laugh and looked sideways at her. 'Don't be embarrassed about last night, Laura. Cal is a real devil with the ladies. I know that well enough.' She gave a satisfied sigh. 'He'll settle down when I come back, though. He'll have everything he needs.'

Laura rode silently. What was there to say, after all? Her dreams had come to nothing as usual but she was used to that. Cal was far beyond her—a cattleman, a rancher. She wasn't even Canadian. He was really a stranger.

Her mind was battling away, telling her that Cal was no stranger, that he wanted her. Wanting wasn't loving, though. She had never felt the warmth of love.

'Oh, God! Look at that!' Felicity stood in the stirrups and then took off fast towards a small stretch of water. There was a horse there, a big one, and Laura couldn't see anything wrong with it.

She followed, and by the time she rode up Felicity had dismounted and was walking round the water, calling to the horse. She turned to Laura with worried eyes.

'This is Cal's best stallion. He's trapped or he would have come when I called. He's got either one leg or two legs tangled in something. If he loses his feet he'll drown. I've seen this before.'

Laura got down from Sky and ran to the edge of the water.

'What should we do?'

'The men will have to get him out. He's too big for us to manage. It's going to take at least three men. By that time it might be too late.'

'Then we'll have to do something ourselves,' Laura said, her practical mind trying to figure out just what could be done.

'You're willing to help?'

'Of course I am.'

'Then I'll ride to the herd and get some of the men. I can go faster than you, so you stay and see that the horse doesn't drown. Go in to him and if he loses his footing, keep his head above water.'

'I'm afraid of water. I can't swim.'

'Oh, for heaven's sake! There's no swimming involved,' Felicity snapped, mounting her horse and wheeling it round. 'Just look. The water's not up to his belly. It won't even reach your shoulders. Get in with him and keep him calm.'

She set off without waiting to argue and she was going faster than Laura had ever done. Seconds later she was out of sight and Laura looked at the horse, who was now anything but calm. He'd been standing quite still when they'd arrived but now he was thrashing about, rolling his eyes, and Laura knew he would fall at any moment.

Cal's horse. She would have been anxious about any animal in danger, but Cal's horse was terribly important to her. She gingerly stepped into the water and made her way towards it.

The water was very shallow by the bank and she managed to move easily at first. Laura felt afraid all the same because somewhere she was going to meet deeper water. She hadn't taken her boots off either and she could feel them filling with water. They were the boots Cal had bought her and they would be ruined.

By the time she reached the horse, the water was up to her chest and she knew one of the reasons he was stuck: there was mud at the bottom of this shallow lake and it was sucking at her feet every time she moved. The water was icily cold and only her determination prevented her from getting out and going to get dry.

The horse didn't appreciate her concern either. When she touched him, he pulled his head away violently. Laura tried to calm him but she couldn't remember his name, even if she had ever been told. She couldn't think about anything except the danger to the horse, the danger to herself and the ever-encroaching mud.

Wild eyes were rolling at her, bared teeth were trying to

bite her, and Laura knew it was just a matter of time before her attempts to avoid him would land her flat on her back in deep, muddy water. By then she wouldn't be able to keep her own head up either.

She didn't hear the pounding of hooves as riders came because by then she was in a sort of dance of death with the huge stallion and he was still stuck. Laura was thankful for that, otherwise she knew he would have gone for her in earnest.

Suddenly, Cal was in the water beside her, his hands on the horse's neck, pushing his head away from Laura. Then there was Mike wading in and taking over from Cal, his dark eyes holding the wild, white-eyed stare of the horse. He began to speak to it, a sort of crooning speech that stilled it instantly. It shivered and stood still and Mike calmed it further by stroking its nose and neck.

Cal lashed his arm around Laura and waded out of the water taking her with him. He was not at all gentle and didn't seem to care whether she was afraid or not. He stood on the bank just looking at her furiously as Tony came up.

'Are you all right, Laurie? You gave us a fright.'

'I—I'm all right,' she said, giving her brother a grateful look because Cal hadn't said a word. The only feeling that was coming from him was one of rage and it seemed to be as wild as the rage the horse had shown.

'I was going to hold his head up out of the water if he fell,' she explained.

Cal didn't say anything to show he had even heard her excuse for being in the water. He simply pointed to Sky. 'Get on your horse and ride back to the ranch,' he snapped. He nodded to Tony. 'Go with her. I'll see her later.'

Laura was dripping with muddy water. It was on her hair where the antics of the horse had splashed her. It was clinging to her clothes and squelching in her boots. Tony took her arm and helped her, but all Laura could think of was that she had risked her life to save Cal's horse and he'd not even asked if she was all right.

Frank and Felicity rode up as Laura reached Sky. Frank looked worried and called to ask how she was but Felicity sat on her horse looking glamorous and healthy. She also looked extremely startled and that annoyed Laura even more. What had the woman expected to find when she'd come back? Felicity had told her to go in with the horse. Had she imagined it could be managed without getting wet and muddy?

She turned for one last look at Cal but he was intent on the horse. His rope went whistling out and settled round the stallion's neck and then Mike was examining the horse's legs. That was the last thing Laura saw as she rode away with Tony.

Tony took her right up to the house and then led Sky to the barn to clean her up and wipe off the saddle. He was looking fairly gloomy himself because Laura had been silent all the way and had snapped at him when he'd spoken.

Now she had to get up to her room without leaving a trail of water and mud. As she opened the door the first person she saw was Biddy, who looked more than shocked at Laura's appearance.

'I went into the water to rescue a horse,' Laura said, almost choking on the words. In fact, now that it was all over she felt shaky and tearful. It had not been a pleasant thing to have to do and she had been frightened all the time. Everything seemed to be catching up with her now— the cold of the water, the rage of the stallion and her own fear of drowning.

Biddy looked at her closely and saw everything. 'Come with me and we'll set you right,' she said quietly. 'There's a shower downstairs. Go straight under the hot water and I'll go up and fetch your robe.'

Laura found herself being pushed towards the downstairs cloakroom with Biddy holding her arm and telling her not to fuss about the mud on the hall floor.

'My boots are ruined,' Laura complained miserably but Biddy handled that too.

'Heavens, girl! If a cowboy's boots were ruined by a bit of water we'd have a stack of them sky-high. I'll wash them and dry them and then give them a good going-over with saddle soap. They'll be better than new, which is more than can be said for my own good boots, slashed open at the hospital and left to finish their days with the trash.'

Laura stood under the hot shower and just let it warm her. She didn't even take her clothes off at first, but when Biddy appeared with her robe and slippers she managed to get her jeans and sweater off and soap herself clean.

Biddy instructed her to leave her clothes where they fell, and by the time she was clean again Laura didn't care what happened to them.

In her own room, Laura sat and dried her hair, thankful that it was now back to its normal colour. She had stopped shivering and now, securely wrapped in her robe, she was beginning to feel better. Biddy brought her a hot drink and took charge of everything and Laura was only too pleased to let her.

She was curled up in a chair, drinking her tea, when she heard Cal come in. Like her he would be frozen and muddy and she spared a thought for Biddy who would have extra washing and another pair of boots to clean. Laura was a little anxious because she knew that, when he was half decent, Cal would be coming to demand explanations.

By the time he came, she had thought things over until she was simmering with annoyance herself, and the fact that he simply walked into her room without knocking was just about the last straw.

Laura didn't get up from her chair, she sat there bristling with irritation and Cal had by no means controlled his temper.

'Now I'll hear the explanations,' he snapped out, 'and they'd better be good.' Furious eyes raked over her. 'And let me tell you, Miss Hughes, that sitting like a schoolgirl with your little toes neatly together and your hair all brushed and shining will not get you out of this latest escapade.'

Laura's hands gripped the arms of the chair and she stared at him angrily. 'What do you mean—escapade? I was trying to save your horse from drowning.'

'You damned near succeeded in getting him shot! The only one likely to drown was you. How much chance do you think you would have had if he'd rolled over onto you? How much chance do you think you'd have had if he'd got his teeth into you?'

'I dodged him quite well,' Laura said huffily. 'Felicity told me to calm him while she rode to get you.'

'She told you to talk to him from the side of the bank but you had to wade in, didn't you? Left to himself he would still have been there when we all rode back. Felicity was as stunned as we were to see you fighting a stallion.'

'His head would have gone under water and he would have drowned,' Laura stated more quietly. She was thinking about her conversation with Felicity, about how she had said that the water would only come to her shoulders at best. There had been no foolish mistake. The only mistake she'd made was to follow Felicity's instructions without thinking.

'You think you're hefty enough to support a full-grown stallion? Listen, you little halfwit, a horse has four legs and in this case only one of them was trapped. If he'd pulled free he would have turned on you after you gave him such a fright.'

Laura shivered and knew she'd had a lucky escape. She looked at Cal's angry face.

'I'm afraid of water. I wouldn't have gone in if Felicity hadn't said it was necessary. Perhaps she's too scared of you to admit the truth, but she told me the horse would probably drown if someone didn't get in with him and hold his head up if he fell.'

He looked at her with narrowed, thoughtful eyes and then simply turned to go out of her room. He tossed his final remark over his shoulder.

'When you come down to dinner tonight we'll sort this all out between us. Either Felicity is lying or you're not safe on a ranch. God knows how you negotiate traffic when you're driving. Have they given you a special notice to stick in the back window—"Laura Hughes. Please pass with care." I don't know how they deal with somebody like you in England.'

As far as Laura was concerned that was it. She sprang up and shouted at him.

'I am not having dinner with somebody who tried to kill me! You can do the questioning yourself. It's bad enough having you say things like that to me without listening to your lady friend simpering with lies and carefully controlled scorn. Climb on the table and entertain her yourself.'

Cal turned and gave her a look scorching with blue-eyed anger. She continued regardless.

'I intend to stay right in this room and read. I'm going to read for the whole of the afternoon and then I'm going to bed. I'm not going to even get changed again. The only way you'll get me down those stairs is if you carry me and

I don't advise such a scenario. I really would shock Miss Rayner then. I'd skittle both of you.'

Cal's eyebrows rose in disbelief and his eyes narrowed even further. 'Don't threaten me, half pint,' he growled. 'I tend to rise to challenges. I expect to see you at dinner and I don't expect to hear any uproar.'

'Expect just what you want,' Laura raged. 'The best thing to expect, however, is nothing, because that's exactly what you're going to get.'

When Cal had stormed off out, Biddy came up and knocked on the door. Knowing that Cal had left the ranch, Laura called out for her to come in. Cal wouldn't have knocked in any case. He seemed to have got into the habit of thinking she didn't need any privacy.

Biddy was trying to control her laughter as she came in. 'I couldn't help hearing that uproar,' she said, grinning all over her face. 'If a man spoke to Cal like that he'd flatten him.'

'Perhaps you didn't hear Cal speak to me,' Laura said tightly. 'I refuse to be treated like an idiot.'

'He was worried about you. He doesn't often lose his temper.'

'No, except with me,' Laura pointed out. 'I don't know what I'm doing here. I'll have to go home in any case. I may as well go now.'

'Well, not today,' Biddy said comfortably. 'What I really came up to say was that if you're hell-bent on staying in your room then I'll get a tray made up for you.'

'No. I don't want to be any trouble, Biddy.'

'You're no trouble, Laura. Best laugh I've had for years. Any trouble I had was keeping my face straight when Cal came thundering downstairs and went out, banging the door. Worth cleaning two pairs of boots any day.'

Laura managed a smile and admired Biddy's new boots

because, true to his word, Cal had presented Biddy with the boots when she was recovered from her fall.

'The new boots look good,' she said, and Biddy gave her a demonstration by doing a quick dance on the spot. It certainly lifted Laura's spirits because Biddy was not everyone's idea of a housekeeper. She had a neat figure and was invariably dressed in tight jeans. Today she wore a purple shirt that was a gaudy contrast to the frizzy red hair she had coloured at the one beauty shop in town. Laura knew this fact because Biddy had confided in her that she had no intention of being old.

'Look,' Laura said. 'If you bring anything up here on a tray you'll be risking a showdown with Cal. He's forbidden it.'

Biddy gave her a smug smile. 'We'll see,' she promised as she went out and Laura gave a resigned sigh. There would be more trouble and that was certain. Cal had decided that she would go down and face his girlfriend but Laura was equally adamant she would not.

Felicity was obviously a fixed part of Cal's life and intended to come back and become an even more fixed part. Laura knew she should be going back to England. She was not about to rage at Felicity in Cal's house. So, as far as she could see, there was nothing for her to do but go down and listen to Felicity glossing over her part in this. Laura was determined not to sit there like a mouse. She would not go down even if she starved.

However, Biddy was a very cunning woman. Just before Cal came home she came up to Laura's room with a tray. It was the dinner for tonight and she told Laura to eat it all up.

'If Felicity Rayner is coming again then I'm off quickly,' she said, looking grim and determined. 'I've put the meal to keep warm so you're the only one getting it while it's fresh and hot.'

'There'll be trouble, Biddy.'

'Don't care. Now you eat this up. You didn't have a bite for lunch and not much breakfast either. We'll just let them think you're starving and, if Cal comes to ask, you can tell him you've eaten already.'

'You're very good to me, Biddy. I seem to have caused a lot of trouble at the ranch.'

'You haven't. Even if you had it wouldn't matter. I like you and I like Tony. So does Cal when he's not in a temper.'

She sailed out and Laura thought the best thing to do was eat while she could. She had a highly likely picture in her mind of Cal storming up here and disposing of her meal.

When she heard him come in she had just about finished it and was filled with amusement that he had been defeated with little trouble. The trouble, of course, would come now.

He never came and demanded her appearance and that put her even more on edge. She was still sitting worrying when Biddy came upstairs with a mile-wide grin on her face and whisked the tray away.

'They're eating all alone,' she said in a stage whisper. 'They're sitting opposite each other, looking like two pot dogs and just about as animated. Never heard anything but if Cal's annoyed—and he looks it—then he's taking it out on that woman.'

Biddy went off, chuckling to herself, and Laura tried her best to read. When she couldn't keep her mind on the printed pages she had a wash again, cleaned her teeth and went to bed.

Before she could actually get into bed, Cal came into her room. She was standing in her short nightie, her robe thrown onto the chair, and she had never felt at such a disadvantage in her whole life.

Cal chose to ignore it all. While she was scrabbling for her robe, trying to get into it and fighting down the flood of heat that covered her face, he was staring at her grimly. Laura could see he thought her an awkward and unusual specimen because that was exactly how he was studying her.

She faced him angrily when she was securely fastened in the robe. 'Come in,' she said loftily. 'I'm ready to receive visitors now. If you could explain your business, I'm sure I can deal with it.'

He didn't rise to the challenge this time. Instead he went on staring at her and then he said, 'I owe you an apology.'

Laura was not about to forgive the way he'd behaved earlier so she kept her aloof attitude and merely nodded in a very condescending way.

'Thank you. I accept your apology. However, I intend to leave here at the first available opportunity. My previous employer did not rage at me. He did not doubt my word and he did not threaten me with physical violence.'

CHAPTER EIGHT

LAURA knew she was deliberately prodding at Cal but she couldn't seem to help it. She saw the blue eyes almost catch fire but she couldn't stop. She felt disappointed when he controlled the ready temper and continued as if she hadn't spoken.

'Felicity admitted, rather reluctantly, that she encouraged you to go into the water to the horse. She said she thought the danger to him was greater than it was. She also said she didn't know you were afraid of water and couldn't swim.'

'How nice to be able to lie easily,' Laura goaded. 'It's something I've never really tried. I could perhaps study the subject when I'm back in England. It has certain advantages as far as I can judge. You can do exactly as you wish and then lie your way out of the consequences.'

'She's going back to Edmonton,' Cal grated.

'Is she? How nice for her. Do you happen to know if she intends to make trouble for everyone there?'

Cal was obviously containing his rage by some super-human effort because he looked as if he refused to be provoked under any circumstance. Laura found that annoying too. It was like trying to get emotion from a mountain face.

'You should come down and eat,' he said coolly. 'Biddy said you'd missed lunch. You could make yourself a meal.'

'I've already eaten,' Laura told him, not without a certain triumph on her face. 'I had my dinner just before you and your guest came into the house. I'll go to bed now and tomorrow we could perhaps speak of my leaving here.

133

There's my salary, which is due at the end of this week as you know, and from that you can deduct anything I owe you.'

Cal seemed to grow bigger right before her eyes and as she turned away in the same imperious manner he pounced. Two long strides had him close and he spun her round, grasping her face between two hard hands.

'Stop it, you sharp-tongued little pest! I've apologised for not believing you. I've sent Felicity on her way. I've come up here to grovel but I'm not about to let you grind me into the dust.'

'I have no wish to grind you into the dust—' Laura began but he didn't let her finish.

'No. You want to provoke me, don't you? You want to make me lose my grip on the situation. You want me to make love to you.'

'I—I don't,' Laura protested, realising that it was what she had hoped for. Now that he was close and now that he obviously knew how she'd been thinking, she didn't want to face the reality of her own actions.

'That's lying, Laura,' he said softly. 'You have such a scorn for liars but you're lying now.'

She couldn't tell him it wasn't true because she knew it was. He looked into her eyes and saw the truth right there.

'All right,' he said quietly. 'I'll make love to you, Laura. I want to and obviously you do too. I can't think of one reason why not.'

Laura could. He didn't love her. There was Felicity who would come back here when he wasn't angry with her. There was England and her brother to help. But most of all there was nothing but desire.

'Please, Cal,' she whispered.

'What does that mean?' He began to plant quick kisses all over her face. 'Do you mean please you or please myself? I can please both of us. I've never had the luxury of taking what I wanted in my whole life but I can have that luxury now because I want you, Laura. I want you more than I've ever wanted anything.'

Before she could reply, before she could think of anything to make him change his mind, his mouth was on hers. He was kissing her with the same heat he had shown before and she felt herself responding in the same way. His tongue was in her mouth, searching the warm darkness, and she felt her heart almost stop when he lifted her hair and nuzzled against her neck as his hands smoothed over her breasts.

'You feel like heaven,' he whispered as his hands skimmed over her. 'You feel like you look—perfect, so slender and soft, so willing in my arms. I want to taste you. I want to taste you all over. Do you want to belong to me, sweetheart? Do you want to be mine right now? I want you so much.'

Laura was like a mindless creature. Her whole world was rapture. From being angry and scornful she was now shaking with feeling, her arms tightly round Cal's neck, and she couldn't think of one reason now why she shouldn't belong to him. This was what she wanted. This was why she had found the courage to goad him.

She was aching with the need to have his hands on her. And they were on her. They were searching her breasts, her back and her thighs. She wanted to feel her skin against him and he knew that too. Without taking his lips from hers he ripped open his shirt and guided her hand to his chest.

'Touch me,' he ordered thickly. 'Touch me, my beautiful Laura.'

Laura's fingers explored his strong muscles, curled into the soft dark hair on his chest and opened out to caress him as he was caressing her. She was a pliant, willing slave in his hands, his to take and take.

Cal was devouring her, tasting her as if he couldn't get enough of her at once. Heat was like a fire between them. Their hearts were pounding almost with the same beat. She couldn't tell which was hers.

And then suddenly it was too much, too soon, too sad.

Laura slid her arms around his waist, rested her face against his skin and began to cry with all the pent-up need of a lifetime without escape. A door had opened but she could not go through it. There was Tony who could never manage without her.

'Laura!' Cal lifted her tear-drenched face and looked down at her, but she couldn't face him. She kept her eyes closed and just let the tears flow.

'I'll be going away,' she sobbed. 'I'll never see you again.'

Cal moved to the chair and sat down, taking her on his lap and gently forcing her head to his shoulder.

'So you're going to leave,' he said heavily. 'You're really going back. I can't make you stay if you want to go home and I know Tony should go when the time comes.' He lifted her face and looked into her eyes, seeing the tears that still refused to stop. 'Stay until he goes, Laura. I promise never to touch you again. I know I promised that before but you're so hard to resist.'

She was still choking on sobs and he put her head back to his shoulder.

'You want me as much as I want you. Walking the line between that desire and staying on the right side is difficult. All the same I want you to stay until Tony goes. I know what you'll have to face in England. Don't you think that both of you have faced enough in your lives? I'll be thinking about you, worrying about you.'

'We're not your worry, Cal,' Laura said, her voice still snatching with tears. 'You've done so much for us. We're not your worry any more.'

He tightened his arms around her, almost crushing her. 'Oh, Laura,' he whispered. 'Stay with me. Stay until you've seen the snow, stay until the spring comes and the snow melts. Stay until the sun makes everything new again. Things might change. Take the chance.'

She raised her head, looking into the brilliant blue of his eyes, and she managed a smile.

'You're tempting me. You know I love being here. England seems to be such a distant place now. I feel much more part of this place. It's wonderful. This house is wonderful and the land and the animals. I understand why Tony wants to be here because I want to be here too.'

Cal's sombre face lit up and his eyes searched her expression. 'You'll stay?'

She gave him a sad little smile. 'I'll stay here until the snow melts and then I'll go home with Tony. Even if this place seems more like home. England is where we live, where we belong.'

'I won't attack you again.'

'You didn't. I provoked you deliberately. I'll not try that again. I know when I've met my match and I know I can't compete against someone like Felicity.'

'She's gone, Laura.'

'She'll be back. She told me so. It may not be soon but she'll come back.'

'I'll post notices around the edge of the ranch,' Cal promised urgently, looking into her eyes. 'I'll learn that damned computer.'

Laura found she was able to laugh. 'You don't have to make rash promises. I'll stay until spring.' She let her head drop to his shoulder thinking she was more content with

Cal than she had ever been in her life. And the thought did
not surprise her. She loved him. He would stay at the front
of her mind always.

'I'm very tired,' she murmured.

'I know,' Cal said softly. 'You've had a busy and unusual day. I'll go and then you can sleep.'

She didn't want him to go. She could have stayed where
she was until the end of time but Laura knew it was just
for now. He wanted her and he was a good man, a kind
man. It would be better for both of them if this episode
could be forgotten.

When Cal had gone she lay in the darkness, too exhausted to cry, too empty to feel anything, but she was not
really unhappy. She would stay and then she would remember. She would remember this place with all its work and
its beauty. She would remember Cal and his strength, his
kindness. Here was where she had discovered love and here
was where it would have to be suppressed as she had suppressed all longings for as far back as she could remember.

Slowly the herd was driven closer to the ranch and there
wasn't much chance of them wandering away again because snow was in the air and everyone could feel it—even
the cattle seemed to know.

Laura worked like mad in the office and helped Biddy
whenever she was allowed to. But mostly she was waiting
for the first fall of snow like everyone else on the Bar W.

She was waiting to go home too. She didn't want to go
but she knew that being here was putting a lot of strain on
her time with Cal. He was back to being the gentle, amusing man she had first met but she often felt his eyes on her
and she knew this state of affairs could not continue as it
was.

She got out of the house most afternoons. She wanted to

exercise Sky and to see as much as possible while she was still here. Laura talked to Mike and Frank too because they had obviously taken a liking to her and it helped to know that she was no longer a stranger. She had made friends here, friends who could have been hers for life—if she had been able to stay.

Tony was now part of the ranch. He had fitted in with no trouble and did his share of work with the men. The fact that he was prepared to ask, if he was insecure about something, and the way he learned quickly had earned him a place with the hardworking ranch hands.

'I almost wish I'd asked Cal to give me a job on the ranch,' she murmured to Mike one day when she was saddling Sky. 'I would have been as much a part of the ranch as Tony is by now.'

Mike shot her a quick look of amusement.

'By now you'd have had two broken legs and a badly strained back. Tony's strong. He can do a day's work with the best of them. Ladies are not cow-hands.'

'I don't see why not,' Laura muttered, tightening the straps of her saddle. 'In the old days women worked side by side with the men.'

'In the old days there wasn't so much paperwork and there were no computers. Women still did women's work. I can't see Cal being able to turn out a good meat pie.'

'You're a chauvinist, Mike,' Laura said with a frown at him as she swung into the saddle. 'Women are all sorts of things now. They're engineers and explorers and even sailors.'

'Yeah? Well, we don't need any bridges built around here and the sea is a good way off. About this exploring business, though, watch your step. There's snow on the way so don't ride out too far. When it comes here, it really comes hard. And don't take any chances either. You may not be a cow-hand but we're all a mite fond of you here on the Bar W.'

Laura flashed him her glorious smile and rode out of the yard. His words had lifted her spirits and she knew she could have made this her home for always had it not been for Cal and her love for him. She could have worked in his office, helped on the ranch and her days would have been happy.

How would she have felt if there had been no Cal, though? Would she still have been content with the wide open spaces, the sea of grass and the high mountains looking down on everything? She just didn't know because Cal *was* here and with him here everything else just fell into place as if she had been born for this life.

In any case, whatever happened, Tony must go back to take up his place at university. He might now be well on the way to being a ranch hand but his life was not here and could never be here. Nor could hers.

Laura had been riding for a good while and, though she kept her eyes on the sky in case snow came, she was simply jogging along thinking. She was riding now beside a small stretch of woodland, with one of the roads into the ranch in front of her, and she was well aware that she had come far enough. She could feel the added cold in the air. It was more pronounced since yesterday.

She reached down and stroked Sky's neck.

'As soon as we reach the trees by the road, we'll turn and go back,' she told the horse. 'We'll not go as far as the fence. But I'll tell you what, we'll go at a fast trot all the way back.'

Sky nodded her head vigorously and seemed to agree, so Laura turned from the trees and met the sharp wind that blew from the Rockies. It was now in her face and trotting fast was a good idea because the wind seemed sharp enough to cut her skin.

She had started urging Sky to move faster when a series of loud bangs close by startled her and startled Sky even more. There had been peace, silence, with only the keen wind in the trees, but suddenly there was loud noise all around them that terrified the horse.

Sky reared up, her front legs pawing the air, and though Laura was now a competent rider she was not prepared for this. It was doubtful if any rider would have been prepared for the sudden change from silence to loud, sharp cracks. Laura fell and Sky took off at a wild gallop, heading for home.

The ground was hard and it hit Laura with a bone-shaking crash as she fell. Blackness was swirling at the back of her mind, everything in slow motion, and she heard a car start up on the road. She turned her head but the pain was too great to allow her to sit up. The pain in her head was almost too bad to allow any movement but she saw the car as it left, passing the fence, going fast and it was Felicity's car.

She came, Laura thought. She came again and now I'm injured. Cal will never believe me this time. The swirling blackness came back and this time Laura could not hold it off.

Cal had just gone into the barn when Sky thundered into the yard. She was sweating, still shivering with fright, and Mike had to catch her.

'Cal!' At Mike's shout Cal came out of the barn and for a second stood still as he saw the riderless mount and knew whose it was.

'Laura,' he whispered, too stunned to move, then he

ran for his horse, which was still saddled. 'Which way did she go?'

The few men who had just come in wheeled their mounts and waited for Cal. Mike simply sprang onto a horse without bothering to saddle up and they all left the yard together.

'I know which way she was heading. She goes there often but she might have turned off,' Mike shouted.

'Split into two parties,' Cal ordered. 'You boys go with Frank, Mike and Tony with me.'

They rode together until they came to a place where Laura could have left the trail and then Cal and Mike continued to the woods in the distance. Tony was white as a sheet. He couldn't keep up with Cal and Mike however much he tried and he was way behind them when they came close to the trees and saw Laura lying on the ground.

Cal left the horse while it was still running and so did Mike but Cal was on his knees beside her first.

'Laura! Laura,' he ordered urgently. 'Wake up! Open your eyes.'

'Nothing broken,' Mike muttered, quickly examining her limbs for breaks. 'It looks as if she came down hard, though, and Sky was running back like the devil was after her.'

Cal wasn't listening. His whole attention was on Laura's face, willing her to be all right. As Tony joined them she murmured fretfully and opened her eyes. She was dazed but her eyes fastened on Cal, who was kneeling beside her and rubbing her hands frantically.

'Wasn't galloping,' she whispered. 'There was a big noise. Squibs.'

Cal looked puzzled and Tony, who was beside him now, said, 'Firecrackers. She means firecrackers.'

'She's right,' Mike said, lifting his head and sniffing the

air. 'I can still smell them. That would have been enough to make any horse rear.'

'Wasn't galloping,' Laura managed painfully. 'I—I didn't gallop, Cal.' She closed her eyes again and Cal spoke to her with the same urgency in his voice.

'No sleeping. You're not to go to sleep, Laura. Stay awake.'

'I hurt,' she complained.

'I know, honey, but you can't go to sleep yet.' When she closed her eyes again Cal spoke more sharply. 'Laura! Do you hear me? I said no sleeping. That's an order.'

She kept her eyes closed. 'Can't bully me. I hurt. Can't order me about.'

'Just wait and see,' Cal threatened. He looked at Mike. 'Do you think it's safe to lift her?'

'I can't find anything broken. It's safer to lift her than leave her lying here. Snow's on its way.' He pointed to the distant mountains and they could all see the haze of white that was blowing from the Rockies.

Cal took off his coat, carefully wrapping her, and when he was in the saddle Mike lifted Laura and put her gently into his arms.

'Ride ahead and call the hospital,' Cal ordered. 'Tony can stay with me. She's got to have someone see to her soon. They'll probably want to keep her in for a day or so even if you're right and nothing's broken.'

Laura opened her eyes. 'No,' she whispered. 'No hospital. Biddy will see to me. I just want to come home.'

'You'll do as you're told,' Cal said tightly.

'I always do,' she whispered, closing her eyes again, and Cal's face softened as he looked down at her.

'Yes,' he said. 'You always do. Just go and let them see to you and then I'll bring you home.'

Tony rode beside them quietly, his face still pale and grim. 'I wonder where home is?' he muttered.

'Home is the Bar W,' Cal said with an equal grimness in his voice. 'It's right in front of us and that's what she's talking about. She knows where home is, Tiger.'

By the time they rode into the yard Mike was able to tell them that an ambulance was on its way from Leviston with a paramedic. Before the others had ridden back it was already in the yard and Laura was carefully lifted onto a stretcher. Tony rode with her and Cal came behind with the Explorer.

'Watch the weather,' Mike warned. 'You might find yourself staying until morning.'

'If she can come out, I'm bringing her home.'

'Okay. If the snow gets bad I'll get out the snowplough. We'll keep the road open if we have to work all night.'

'Laura wants to come home,' Cal said, looking up at his friend.

'I heard her. That answers one of your questions at any rate.'

'Does it? After a fall like that and lying in the cold, I think anywhere with a warm bed and a hot drink is home.'

He drove out, following the ambulance, and Mike stared after them all with dark, thoughtful eyes. Then he looked at the sky and the distant mountains. There was no fall of snow as yet and it might hold off until nightfall, but it would surely come then with a vengeance. Wherever Laura counted as home, she was here for the foreseeable future. She was definitely here until the snow cleared a little. Time was a remarkable thing. They would have to see what it brought.

'Going to need the plough by morning,' Frank said, coming up closer.

'We'll maybe need it tonight. If Laura can come out, Cal will bring her home.'

'Heard that,' Frank murmured. 'Reckon I'll go up and tell Biddy. Tricky state of affairs, according to Biddy.'

'Yeah,' Mike muttered, but his mind wasn't on that sort of thing. 'Laura often rides up to the trees. The back road to town runs just by where we found her. There were used firecrackers where she fell. They were new enough for me to smell them. Somebody was there.'

'Laura's too good now to simply fall off a horse,' Frank agreed. 'We should maybe look for tracks.'

'I'll look,' Mike said. 'While you're talking all this over with Biddy, just keep an eye on the weather because Laura wants to come back and Cal will bring her even if he has to carry her through snowdrifts.'

Nothing was broken. Mike's diagnosis was correct. Laura had concussion and she was badly shaken. Cal and Tony were told that the shock would take a while to wear off and the concussion would give her bad headaches for a few days.

'She's lucky,' the doctor said when Cal had explained the circumstances of her fall. 'A toss like that could have killed her.'

Tony was very silent as they made their way to the ranch with Laura lying in the back as comfortable as they could make her.

'What about the firecrackers?' he said quietly to Cal. 'Laura doesn't imagine things and Mike said he could smell them.'

'I know. I haven't forgotten. It seems to me she's had too many accidents lately. Let's just get her into bed and then I'll tackle the mysterious firecrackers.'

'They couldn't have set themselves off,' Tony muttered.

'They couldn't. Leave it to me. Let's just be thankful she's all right. That injection they gave her at the hospital calmed the pain down. I've got tablets for later. Biddy will get her into bed and then it's just a matter of time.'

'Should I move back to the house?'

'Please yourself. It's up to you, but Laura will be guarded well until I get to the bottom of this trouble.'

'I know. Reckon I'll stay in the quarters,' Tony decided after a long look at Cal. 'Don't want Laura to think I'm fussing.'

Cal smiled secretly. Tony was even talking like the boys now.

'She'll be well looked after, Tiger.' He looked up at the sky, which was darkening towards evening now. 'Come morning you'll see what real snow is like.'

'And what real cold is like,' Tony surmised. 'I've never been fascinated by snow but Laura loves it. She's like a child about it and never cares if she's trudging to work through the slush it leaves behind.'

'She'll see this without trudging through slush.' Cal glanced in the mirror to check on her but she was sleeping, although her face was still showing signs of pain. He had a picture of her trudging through slush and enjoying it, making happiness where she could.

Would Charlie have made her happy if he'd stayed at home? He'd made plenty of other people happy while Laura had faced things no child should have to face. He didn't know now whether Charlie was an old so and so or not.

Laura slept through the getting-into-bed part. Marge and Biddy saw to her and settled her comfortably.

'She's bruised all over,' Biddy told Cal when she came downstairs. 'It's going to be a few days before she's over this.'

When she went off to see to the dinner, Mike walked in and nodded to Cal, making it clear he had news. When they were in the office with the door closed, Mike opened his hand and showed Cal the remains of the firecrackers.

'I went out there as soon as you'd gone,' he said. 'Didn't want a fall of snow to cover any tracks.'

'Were there any, with the ground being so hard?'

'Plenty in the woods where the frost lingered. Somebody came by car and parked at the side of the road leading to town.'

'What sort of tracks in the woods?'

'A woman's tracks,' Mike said. 'Course, it could be a small man, but he'd have to be light and slim. I've never seen a man like that round here.' He looked at Cal and walked out and Cal stared grimly after him. He hadn't seen a slender man about either. He lifted the phone and called the hotel. He knew who was staying there at the moment and the sooner she was back to Edmonton, the sooner Laura would be safe.

When Laura woke in the night, Cal was sitting in the chair by her bed. He seemed to be sleeping and she was so disorientated that she couldn't work out why he was there. When she tried to move, however, pain shot through her head and her back felt as if it were breaking. She remembered then with no trouble at all. She'd been tossed to the hard ground when Sky had reared.

Her slight cry of pain as she tried to move brought Cal's eyes open at once and he came to the bed immediately.

'I've got a terrible headache,' she whispered.

Cal nodded. 'I expected that. I've got some tablets for you. They gave me them at the hospital.'

'My back hurts too. I wouldn't mind a dose of Mike's ointment, even if he had to rub it in himself.'

'I don't think it will come to that,' Cal said, smiling down at her. 'We'll see what tomorrow brings. You hit the ground very hard when Sky tossed you off.'

Laura lay very still and watched him anxiously. 'I saw Felicity's car,' she whispered.

'I know. Mike found her tracks. He found her tracks in the wood too and he brought back the remains of the fire-crackers.'

'She'll come again.'

'She won't. I rang Al Bisley's place but she'd left on the last train out. By now, Felicity is back in Edmonton. She can't come back here and she knows it. Besides,' he added, wanting to bring a smile to her pale face, 'by morning there'll be snow.'

He got the smile even if it was a painful one.

'I love snow.'

'I know, Tiger told me. Bet there's no snow in England to match this, though. Get better and I might help you to build a snowman. Might make you a sledge too.'

Laura managed to laugh, but it cost her an effort and brought another groan of pain that had Cal fetching the tablets and raising her head carefully while she took them with a small drink of water.

'Try to sleep now,' he said, lowering her gently to the pillows.

'There's no need for you to stay here and watch me,' Laura whispered as she closed her eyes.

'Somebody has to watch you and I voted myself in.'

'You'll be tired tomorrow.'

Cal stroked back her hair. 'I voted myself out of tomorrow too. Mike will take the helicopter up if it's needed.'

'I like Mike,' Laura muttered as the tablets began to ease her pain and make her sleepy.

'Sure you do, honey. He's my brother. He's going to do the work while I play in the snow.'

Laura went to sleep and, after watching her for a minute or two, Cal settled himself back in the chair and closed his eyes. That was how Laura saw him in the morning, with his black hair falling over his forehead and his neck at an uncomfortable angle.

Her own head felt strange and painful but she could see the white light on the ceiling and the stillness was almost total. Snow had fallen and she felt the same excitement she had felt as a child. She disobeyed all orders and carefully got out of bed.

The pain hit her at once but she bit at her lips to stop the groans and crept towards the window, holding the furniture to help her along. She had waited for this and nothing was going to stop her from looking.

Cal slept like a cat, however, and the moment she started across to the window his blue eyes shot open and he was on his feet.

'Where do you think you're going? You're not supposed to move out of that bed for another two days.'

Laura hung onto the dressing table and pleaded, with little hope of success. 'I want to see the snow. I know it's come at last. Just one little look and then I'll go back to bed and rest.'

When he looked at her severely she tried another tack. 'Oh, please let me, Cal.'

He shook his head at her and gave her a rueful glance. 'Think you can get round me easily, don't you?'

'I know I can't,' Laura whispered.

'Funny how you always manage to do it, though, isn't it?' He came towards her and lifted her gently into his arms. 'Come on, then. One quick glance and then you're back in that bed.' Laura rested her sore head on his shoulder and he looked down at her. 'Even that's not going to get you more than a minute,' he warned. 'We're following strict rules here and I'm sticking to them, so no trying to wheedle round me.'

Laura managed a smile and rested her head more comfortably, snuggling into his warmth.

'That's wheedling,' Cal said sternly, 'and it won't get you a second longer at the window.'

When he pulled the curtains open, Laura gasped at the sight that met her eyes. Everything was a dazzling white. Every hollow was filled in. She was looking at a fairyland where snow hung from the trees and covered the ranch buildings, lying on the rooftops like a thick blanket.

There was no sign of the yard at all but here and there were cattle, darker shadows on the white pasture. Everything was pristine, untouched, as if the whole world were new.

'It's wonderful,' Laura sighed. 'Oh, how I wish I could run out into that snow and enjoy it.'

'You'll have the chance to enjoy it,' Cal said quietly. 'This is only a slight fall. The boys haven't even bothered to get the road cleared and it's time they moved.'

'Will you be going down to shout at them?'

'Stop putting about the impression that I spend my days roaring at people,' Cal ordered. 'One minute I'm so good to you and the next I'm a tyrant. My reputation will be shot to pieces soon.'

'It won't. Will you have to take the helicopter up today?'

'Not too likely. Mike might take a spin around and see what's happening but he might decide to leave things.'

'When you go up, can I come with you?'

'Honey, I wouldn't dare,' Cal muttered, turning back to the bed. 'You've nearly been killed twice and that was at ground level.'

'It wasn't my fault.'

'No, it wasn't.' Cal put her into bed and pulled the covers up around her. He looked into her face, which was now paler than ever. The front door banged as Biddy arrived and as they both heard it Cal asked, 'How about a little breakfast now?'

'I couldn't.'

'Not even if I promise to take you up in the helicopter when you're better?'

'I'll eat some toast,' Laura promised. Her face was smiling now and Cal stood looking down at her before he strode out of the room.

'There,' he said softly. 'Don't tell me you can't get round me. You don't even have to try.'

CHAPTER NINE

LAURA was in bed for two more days. Biddy brought all the news and saw to her personal comfort. Marge and Helen visited and stayed to gossip and one evening she had a visit from Mike, Frank and Tony.

Of course, Tony had come each day, stayed to have dinner with Cal and come to bid her goodnight, but this was a special visit with them all coming to see how she was.

Laura felt tears sting at the back of her eyes as they gathered round the bed. She had never had so many people who cared about her and she could see they cared about Tony too. There was an easy comradeship here and he was part of it.

They treated her like a delicate princess and Cal, coming in later, thought she looked like that. A delicate princess with her courtiers round her. She looked too fragile to take the rough and tumble of life out here, too easily hurt and damaged. It took a lot of effort to keep the smile on his face.

'This brother of yours is a real card-sharp,' Frank told her. 'He can remember every card that's been played. Don't know what he wants a wage for. He can clean the boys out any time.'

'I warned you. You shouldn't have taught him,' Mike remonstrated. 'He learns everything too quickly. Anybody with any sense would know he could learn poker in two shakes.'

'Hey! I offered to give everything I won straight back,' Tony complained.

152

'Think the boys would have been as kindly if you'd lost?' Frank asked. 'They were looking to have a good laugh while they cleaned you out.'

'Then I wouldn't have played again.' Tony grinned. 'I'm working to save up for when we get back to England. There'll be college looming up soon enough.'

'Looking forward to it?' Frank squinted across at Tony.

'In a way. I'm enjoying it here. I feel at home here but we have to go back eventually.'

They stayed talking for a lot longer, telling Laura about the new fall of snow and promising more to come, but the earlier talk had robbed her of her smiles. Tony felt at home here and so did she. She caught Cal's eyes on her and was even more depressed. He was looking cold and hard again.

When the others went, Cal came back up to her room and she looked at him solemnly. 'I suppose you think Tony is as much a gambler as my father,' she said. 'He isn't. In fact he's never played cards before and I wish he wouldn't now.'

Cal sat in the chair and sighed heavily. 'I don't think anything of the sort. Why should you assume my mind is running in that direction?'

'It sounded like history repeating itself. But Tony is very clever. He got a place at university a year ahead and he could have got one two years ago. He's a brilliant mathematician. They shouldn't have taught him to play poker. He remembers everything.'

'You're only arguing with yourself, Laura. I've been hearing about this for weeks. The boys think it's some sort of magic. And I'll tell you this, Charlie wouldn't have offered to pay back their losses. When Charlie played cards he was in deadly earnest. Tony is showing them like a magician with tricks. The ranch hands are falling over themselves to try and outwit him. There's a party every night in the cookhouse when they've eaten. They're still talking about it when they ride out the next day. If it wasn't for Tony they'd be up half the night. He's the one who tells them when it's over.'

Laura reached for her dressing gown and slid from the bed.

'Where are you going?'

'I'm getting up. I don't like this card playing.'

'You're going to go out, struggle through the snow to the cookhouse and lay down the law?'

'Of course not! I'm just tired of being in bed.' She fastened her robe tightly around her while Cal watched with narrowed eyes. 'I'm better now. I want to get up.'

He just sat in the chair and watched her and she felt grieved and lonely for no other reason than that Tony was one of the boys and she was treated like an invalid. Everything was mixed up in her head, the happiness churning round with the tears, and Cal was sitting there looking handsome, dark and wonderful.

'Come here,' he said softly.

'I don't want to. I'm going to walk about. You can go because I don't need watching any more.'

'Come here,' he repeated and she trailed slowly towards him, her head down and her eyes hidden from him.

When she was standing in front of the chair he reached out and took her hand. 'What's the matter, Laura? You're crying inside.'

'I'm not.'

'Yes, you are. I know you. I know how that mind works and now it's sad. Tell me what's wrong and I'll make it right. I'll make it go away.'

'There are some things that even you can't do,' Laura whispered.

'Try me,' he said, pulling her onto his lap. 'Just tell me why you're so sad and I'll fix it.'

'You can't fix everything.' Laura rested her head on his shoulder and he smiled against her glittering hair.

'You belong there, don't you? You belong with your head on my shoulder. You put it there when we first met. You fell asleep in the car and snuggled against me.'

Laura started to move and he stopped her at once. 'Shh,' he said softly. 'Just be quiet with me for a moment. You need this and so do I.'

'It's temporary,' Laura whispered.

'I know. I know more than you think. I heard Tony talking about England. I heard the bit about saving up for you both to go home. And I know what this place means to you. You're torn between one thing and another. You want to stay here but you want to go back with Tony. We both know that he'll go and you'll go with him.'

Laura looked up with tears in her eyes. There was longing on her face too and Cal's blue eyes studied her and then he held her carefully and kissed her. He was very tender, his lips just drifting over her soft mouth.

'Nobody is going to hurt you,' he whispered against her face. 'Nobody is going to hurt you ever again.'

His words were the only thing that was needed to bring the tears she had so carefully controlled. They fell steadily down her cheeks and she raised her lips to his when his mouth came back to hers. He was gentle, careful, tender and the care left Laura filled with longing. Her tears mingled with his kisses.

'Please love me now, Cal,' she begged. 'You said you wanted me. Want me now.'

His arms tightened but he was strictly in control of himself. 'Oh, I want you, Laura,' he said quietly. 'But I'm not about to make love to you. I know you'll feel the need to go when Tony goes and I couldn't take the wrench if you belonged to me. You couldn't take it either, not a girl like you. Besides,' he added, suddenly grinning down at her, 'you've been very ill. You just couldn't cope with the way I feel.'

Laura sat up straight. 'You're laughing at me!'

'I'm not. I'm trying to keep us both sane. Making love has consequences and I'm not certain that you could face those consequences.' He cupped her face in his warm hand and stared into her eyes. 'If I made love to you, there would be no chance of going, believe me. When the time came, Tony would be getting on that plane all alone.'

Laura stared up at him and he stared back into her eyes. 'Think about it before you beg me to make love to you again,' he said quietly. 'You're more than ready for me and I told you once before, I'm used to having my own way.'

He put her on her feet and unfastened the robe with swift fingers. Then he lifted her and strode to the bed, putting her under the covers before looking down at her with suddenly dangerous eyes.

His voice softened to a low murmur. 'Next time you tempt me, I'll give in. Remember that.'

He walked quietly out of the door and Laura closed her eyes, shivers running over her hot skin. It was true she had tempted him, she had begged him, but he had reached for her and kissed her. He had known how she felt too and how she still wished to protect Tony even though he showed every sign of being a man now.

Cal didn't know one thing, though. He didn't know she loved him and if he made love to her it would break her heart. He was wiser than she was. He knew it would come to nothing in the end and he was right, she couldn't take that. Walking off with a cheerful wave then and going back to England was not something she could ever face.

In the night, more snow fell and Laura awoke to the sound of the plough clearing the roads close to the ranch. When she went to the window she saw the helicopter being pushed out of one of the huge sheds and in a minute Cal was walking across to it.

He was dressed for the cold with a sheepskin jacket and thick gloves. Mike, similarly dressed, joined him after a second or two and they both climbed into the machine.

As it started and moved upwards and away, Laura saw that Cal was flying it. He did it as he did everything else, skillfully and competently, and as she watched the machine hovered and then turned towards the flat, open stretches of snow-covered prairie. Soon it was out of sight and Laura turned back to her room with a sigh.

Today she was going downstairs but there was no joy in it. Cal was somewhere else, flying over his land, searching for cattle in trouble or any that had been foolish enough to wander off. He wouldn't be thinking of her. He was part of the ranch, part of the land and she was just an unusual episode in the wide scope of his days. When she was gone he would slowly forget her.

She pulled herself out of the misery and dressed. There would be work in the office, neglected while she'd been in bed, and she was not about to spoil her remaining time here with gloom. If Cal had loved her she would have stayed and let Tony travel to England alone but Cal had never said that.

He was attracted to her, he cared about her, but that was all. She was still only a guest here, a working guest, and she would have to leave soon. If there had been no fall of snow she would have gone as soon as she felt fit because staying would only make things worse in the end.

When the helicopter came in and Cal came back to the

house she was already working in the office. He came in and stopped, looking startled to see her there.

'I was all set to do some of the work myself,' he said. 'I didn't think you'd feel up to it.'

'I feel fine for this sort of thing. It's not as if it's hard. I thought you would be busy all day.'

'We did the hard work before the snow came,' Cal reminded her, bending to stir up the fire that brought a warm glow to the room. 'Now there are just a certain amount of jobs to get through each day, providing nothing of importance happens.'

'You came back for lunch?'

'Sure. No need to take it on the hop now. Mike and I dropped feed to the cattle that wandered a way off. The boys will feed the ones close to the ranch.' He sat in the chair by the fire. 'In other words, nothing much is happening. I get to take it easy.'

A few days later, after lunch Biddy spoke to Cal very quietly.

'I'd like to clear Josh's room out today,' she said, keeping a wary eye on him. 'It's got to be done some time, all the drawers and cupboards. You've got to think about what you want to do with his things, Cal.'

For a moment, Cal looked very tight-faced and Biddy obviously expected a tongue-lashing. He calmed down, though, and gave her a smile. 'It's time, I suppose. You can do it, Biddy. Leave the photographs just where they are but you can get rid of everything else. Don't throw out any of his special things, though. I'll store them.'

When Biddy left the room Cal sat in silence for a minute and then he said, 'It's funny. When he died I wanted to nail his door shut and never go in there again. Now I feel different. I suppose that while I've been explaining to you about Charlie I've explained Josh to myself. Now, I miss him. When he was alive I just wanted him to keep away, to stay down at Blue Moon with Charlie and keep out from under my feet.' He gave a soft laugh. 'I'm even calling that damned cabin by the fancy name they gave it.'

'Time sorts things out,' Laura said softly. 'It comes like the snow and covers all the hard, sharp patches. You're left with a picture of the good things.'

'Are you left with a picture of the good things at home?' Cal asked, looking across at her.

Laura turned away as she answered. 'I can't really remember many good things. I can only remember duty and worry and trying to laugh my way above it. There were no hard, sharp patches to cover. There was just dreariness.'

'Is it dreary here?'

'Oh, no!' Laura smiled enchantingly as she turned her face back to look at him. 'It's exciting and different every day. I've never really known so many nice people and the scenery is wonderful.'

'Stay here, then.'

The smile died on Laura's face. 'You know I can't do that. Even if I wanted to, this is not my home.'

'When you had the bad fall you said you wanted to come home. You didn't say you wanted to *go* home,' Cal reminded her.

'You can't hold something against a person who's had a bang on the head,' Laura pointed out.

Cal just looked at her and they didn't get the opportunity to continue the conversation because the door banged and Tony came in grinning. 'We've finished for the time being,' he said to Cal. 'Roy's shuffling the cards so I got out while I still could.'

'Well, it's safer here, then,' Cal said, standing and moving to the door. 'Stay for dinner and meanwhile you can catch up on the news with Laura.' He walked out and Laura had a hard time trying to keep a welcoming smile on her face for her brother. She realised that nowadays her whole world revolved around Cal. When he wasn't there, she felt lonely no matter who was in the room.

Just before dinner, when Tony had gone back down to his quarters for a while and Laura was sitting alone, Cal came back in, looking sombre. He had a box in his hand. It was a long box, the sort of thing that deeds were left in, and his eyes went straight to Laura's.

'Biddy found this at the back of one of the drawers in Dad's room. There's a letter I'd like you to read.' He handed it to her. 'Maybe I should have searched before but I had no idea this was there.'

When Laura opened the letter and saw Cal's name she looked up at him in surprise.

'But it's a letter to you. This will be private and nothing to do with me.'

Cal turned away impatiently. 'I've read it. I want you to read it now. It may be written to me but it concerns you and Tony. Read it.'

He started to pace about the room and, after watching him for a second, Laura had a terrible premonition that this was the end of her time with Cal. She didn't want to know what was in the letter Josh Wexford had left for his son.

'Read it,' Cal suddenly bit out. 'There's nothing to be scared of. The news is good, Laura. It solves all your problems.'

He didn't look as if it would solve anything but Laura stopped gazing into his eyes and turned to the letter. It was a letter from a man who had loved his son and Laura felt tears sting at the back of her eyes when she read it. It explained so much about the man who had loved so well that he couldn't continue when his wife died. Laura knew why Josh had brought Mike to the ranch now, to be a brother to Cal, someone who would stand beside him when his father had gone.

It explained how he had needed her father too, needed his companionship to get him through the days. She knew, even if she had not known before, why Josh Wexford had allowed Blue Moon to be built. When he spoke of her father there was the amused indulgence in his letter that Cal himself always showed.

Josh wrote finally:

I know you thought Charlie was a tearaway, but he never stopped thinking about his family. He couldn't go back to them but he never forgot them. When he came here, he had quite a bit of money and he saved it. He built Blue Moon and insisted on paying for it, then he lived each day by his wits. He rode with the hands when he could. He killed the odd deer, caught fish and took the boys for their wages if he was short.

All the time he had money but he hung onto it for his children. I kept it in this box for him and I'm leaving it with you, Cal, because I know you'll see that they get it. There's a girl called Laura and a boy called Tony. They may need help and I know you'll give it because you live by a code of your own and I'm proud of you.

Laura looked up at Cal and he was watching her intently. 'So my father remembered us,' she whispered. 'He didn't forget either of us.'

'He didn't forget. I don't know why he never came back to you. My father found it hard to live without my mother, maybe Charlie found it equally hard to live *with* your own mother. Whatever the reason, he didn't forget you.' Cal opened the box again and held up the notes inside. 'I counted it,' he said quietly. 'Mostly it's in American bills and there's the equivalent of twenty thousands pounds in English money. Either he made that in the oil fields or he added to it by going short while he was here. Whatever he did to get it, he hung onto it for you and Tony.'

Cal put it by Laura on the coffee-table, more money than she had ever seen in her life. She just stared at it in a daze. Now they were not penniless. Now they would be able to go home and settle with little problem. It wasn't a fortune but it would mean that they could be reasonably comfortable in England.

They could rent a decent house. With the money they had earned on the Bar W they would be safe. She could get a job with little difficulty and Tony would go to university with enough money to make him comfortable there.

So why was she almost horrified?

There was no excuse for staying here any longer. The heavy fall of snow had not yet come and she knew Tony wasn't wild about the bitter cold. He had some studying to do before he went to university too. All his books were in England. She felt thoughts running frantically through her mind, and when she looked up Cal had left the room.

He was quiet at dinner time, back to being a hard man who lived a hard life, and Laura knew the only reason he made the effort to speak was because Tony was there. Even so, he said nothing about the letter and the unexpected money. Finally, Laura had to tell Tony herself and she quietly related the contents of the letter and the box filled with bank notes.

Tony was stunned. He sat in silence for a minute and then he said, 'He actually remembered my name?'

That he should have focused on that one fact when there was much more involved hit Laura badly. She realised all over again that they had only each other and that Tony relied on her as he had relied on her all his life. He wasn't yet eighteen and, although he now looked a man, the ties that bound her to her duty were too strong to be broken yet.

She glanced up at Cal in time to see a similar recognition on his face. It was only a fleeting expression but it was there and when the blue eyes met her own he gave a slight smile and nodded to her.

Tony came out of his preoccupied silence, his enthusiasm rising by the minute. 'This means we'll be able to get a nice place to live, Laurie. We've both saved a lot here and with the money Dad left us we'll be comfortable.'

'That's true,' Laura agreed. 'It gives us the security we lost when we decided to come out here. You've had your chance to be a cowboy and I've had the chance to live in a beautiful place.'

'Maybe we should go back while there's still no big fall of snow,' Tony deliberated thoughtfully. 'I've got a lot of books to read before university starts next year. I could get down to it now because I won't need a job.'

Laura's heart sank but she managed to smile. 'I've been thinking that myself. There's also the problem of finding a house and deciding where we want to live.'

'According to Mike,' Cal said quietly, 'this week will bring a heavy fall of snow. The roads will be kept open but there'll be a bit of chaos to begin with.'

'Then we should leave soon.' Laura said briskly. She was determinedly stifling any other feelings, making sure that neither Cal nor Tony should know how she felt. 'We could go the day after tomorrow.'

'Good idea. What do you think, Cal? There's not much I can do on the ranch at the moment.'

'Not much,' Cal agreed. 'By the time the snow goes

we'll all have got used to managing without you.' He was smiling at Tony, looking amused and indulgent, but his words sank deeply into Laura. When the spring came he would have forgotten about her too. Things would be back to normal as if she had never been here at all.

Tony went down to the cookhouse to tell everyone about their Eldorado but all the things she had laughingly told Tony before they'd come here now brought her nothing but misery. Her father had not found a kingdom where he was king. She was not a princess. She was already in the place she had always wanted to be. Here she had friends, people who cared about her. Here she had happiness.

When she was in her room later, Laura felt too restless and miserable to get into bed. She wandered round the lovely room touching things she would never see again. She stood looking out of the window. The lights were on and she could see the snow, crisp and hard where it had not been cleared. The trees were heavy with snow and she would never see this wonderland again.

Cal just walked in and came across to her.

'I never heard you knock,' she said vaguely, not even looking round.

'I didn't,' he murmured, standing behind her and gazing out at the snow. 'Walking in here to you has just become a habit. When you're gone I'll have to break the habit or I'll be walking in on some poor, unsuspecting guest.'

'Some poor, unsuspecting female,' Laura corrected quietly.

Cal lashed his arms round her and pulled her back against him. 'I don't think so,' he said intensely. 'This will always be Laura's room. I'll keep it for when you come to visit. You won't forget the Bar W, even if it fades to a small memory at the back of your mind.'

Laura turned in his arms and looked up at him. 'Will you forget me, Cal?' she whispered.

'Never,' he said, his blue eyes drowning her. 'I'll see you every time I ride out alone. I'll think of you every time I have dinner, every time I go into my office, every time I look up the stairs. When I pass this room I'll look in, just in case you've come back.'

Laura's lips trembled as she attempted to smile and he ran his finger along the soft line of them. Watching their velvet smoothness.

'If ever I kiss anyone,' he whispered, 'I'll imagine it's you.'

Laura flung her arms around his neck and felt the strong hands at her waist, urging her closer. She didn't want to go. She loved him so much and once again she was torn both ways between duty and happiness.

'You said that the next time I begged, you would just give in,' she choked. 'Make love to me, Cal.'

He drew back to look at her and she was watching him with dark, tear-filled eyes. He wiped her tears away with his thumbs, watching her cheeks as more tears fell.

'I said something else,' he reminded her huskily. 'I said I wouldn't let you go if I made love to you. I told you Tony would be going back alone.'

Tears streamed down her face. 'Don't let me go,' she begged.

'I can't,' he said urgently, pulling her closer. 'If you want to go, I'll ride to Blue Moon and keep you there. I'll go up into the mountains and build a cabin where nobody can find you.'

All the time he was speaking his hands were undressing her with almost feverish need and Laura was pulling at his shirt, running her hands over the smooth strength of his chest. She was crying and laughing at the same time and he was placing swift, urgent kisses on her mouth and her face.

'We would starve,' she whispered.

'Mike would ride up with food for us,' he murmured against her silken skin. 'He wouldn't tell a soul and the whole of the country would be searching for you. When the snow melted I would just move you higher into the mountains.'

'Kidnapped,' Laura whispered, kissing the smooth muscles of his arms, trembling when her last garment fell to the floor.

'Kidnapped,' he agreed, lifting her against his warmth and burying his lips in her neck. 'I wanted you the moment I saw you and now I've got you.' He put her on the bed and began to undress, looking down at her the whole time. 'We're pretty wild up here. Far from civilisation, a good way from the law. I could just say that you'd gone back to England.'

Laura was watching him with wide eyes, her body trembling. He looked so magnificent, golden and tall, his black hair gleaming in the lamplight.

'Mike would tell everyone,' she whispered, joining in the sensuous story.

'Mike is my brother. He would keep our secret,' Cal said, leaning over her, trapping her with his gaze, and Laura felt herself drowning in his eyes, mesmerised as she had always been by the blue that looked like a reflection of the sky.

She reached up slowly to touch him and Cal couldn't keep it up any more. He groaned low in his throat and came down to her, folding her in his arms.

'It's a wonderful idea,' he said thickly, 'but reality is much more wonderful. After tonight you belong to me completely. After tonight you'll have no right to ask me to knock on your door.' He nuzzled against her neck and whispered in her ear. 'After tonight I own every bit of you.'

Laura arched against him, trying to get closer. 'You own so much already,' she gasped as his mouth caressed her tight breasts.

'And I'd trade it all for you, sweetheart,' he said huskily. 'Every blade of grass, every acre of the ranch, everything I own in exchange for you.'

He pushed her gently away to trail kisses over her body, holding her still when she cried out in delight and tried to get closer, but his hands followed the path of his lips, holding her fast and she felt as if her whole body were enclosed in flame.

She pulled her arms free and her hands tangled in his black hair, her moans of pleasure lost in his mouth as his lips came back to hers. His mouth was fiercely possessive and she was mindless with pleasure, tossing restlessly beneath him.

Cal tore his mouth free as she began to make small, demanding cries of passion. 'Laura, sweetheart! Do you know what you're doing?' he gasped. 'I've no control left. Tell me now if you want to stop.'

'No! No!' She clutched him closer, placing frantic kisses on his skin. 'Tomorrow I'll have nothing. Tonight I have you. Don't move away, Cal. Please!'

'Oh, Laura, darling. I don't think I could, even if you begged me.'

He possessed her swiftly and hungrily, silencing her cry of shock with warm, passionate lips. Heat rushed through her and an excitement she had never known, never imagined. It reached every part of her, making her feel faint, and when she opened her eyes she was drowning in blue again as Cal looked down at her.

'Now you're mine,' he whispered. His strong hands

swept her over, lifting her closer, and then he began to move inside her and Laura's eyes closed with the power of it. She drifted on the edge of a dream until the whole night seemed to shatter into a shower of golden stars. She went higher than the snow-covered mountains, higher than the sky, and fell back to earth enclosed in the strength of his arms.

Cal rested his dark head against her breasts, his breathing erratic as she lay limp beneath him. She felt relaxed, almost lifeless, but filled with a joy she had never known. Her eyes were still closed when he lifted his head to look at her.

'Laura.' His fingers traced her face, lingering against the soft, silky skin. 'Laura, sweetheart,' he whispered urgently. When she opened dark, liquid eyes and looked up at him, a spasm of near pain crossed his face. 'Let me stay with you all night. Let me hold you in my arms in this room. Give me that to remember.'

Laura pulled him fiercely to her, loving him with every fibre of her being. At this moment he seemed so lost and she wanted to be everything he needed.

Soon they were entwined together again, until they were wrapped in a world of passion, joined in a frenzy of rapture that took Laura to the top of the mountains again. She fell asleep with Cal's kisses on her face and neck, his murmurs of endearment in her ears and the strong, brown hands that could vanquish anything were soft and soothing on her heated skin.

In the morning he was gone and Laura lay still, watching the light of the snow on the ceiling and feeling that she had dreamed the ecstasy that the night had brought. Her clothes were folded neatly on the chair, though, and Cal's head had left its impression on the pillow beside her.

He had begged to stay with her in this room. He had said he wanted to remember. Well, she had given him that during the long night and now she had to go home and leave him. She had to take up her duty again and leave Cal here. If he asked her to stay she would stay and never leave, but he would not ask. He had not asked even in the night when they'd been fast in each other's arms.

He agreed with her going. She had seen it on his face at dinner when Tony had talked about the things that needed to be done in England. Laura had no doubt that he wanted her to stay but he didn't love her enough to keep her here, to insist on his right to be with her. And always there was her duty to her brother. He did not have Cal's strength of will. Tony could never manage without her.

CHAPTER TEN

LAURA went down to breakfast and met Cal's eyes coura-
geously. There would be no pleading from her. She had
never pleaded for anything in her life and she was not about
to beg now for something she could never have.

He was silent and thoughtful throughout breakfast and
then he said, 'Get something warm on and I'll take you for
that ride in the helicopter. The sun is shining on the snow
so you'll need some dark glasses.'

Before she would have been as pleased as a child but
now she knew it was one last thing he could do for her
and, looking at his face, Laura recognised that. He was
indulging her as he had indulged her since she had been
here.

She nodded and went to get the jacket he had bought
her. It was light but very warm, the hood lined with fur.
He had bought her a cap too and she pulled it onto her fair
head and looked at herself in the mirror.

Everything was a memory of Cal. Everything would always be a memory of him. She tightened her lips and faced
facts as she had always done. She was going back to
England, taking Tony back and seeing to the things he
needed, but now it was a duty she could only face with
despair.

On the stairs she met Biddy who looked at her with re-
proachful eyes. 'Cal says you're going tomorrow.'

'Yes, Biddy. We have to go before the deep snow ar-
rives. Tony has a lot to do before university starts.'

'Wish I'd never told Cal what I found in Josh's room,'

Biddy said miserably. 'Wish I'd just kept quiet and left it there.'

'We would still have gone, Biddy. We live in England.'

'What's wrong with here?' Biddy asked fretfully. 'You've fitted in here real good. What are we supposed to do without you?'

'Oh, Biddy, I'll miss you.' Laura hugged Biddy close and then hurried down the stairs. Cal was waiting at the bottom of the steps and he said nothing. He had obviously heard but he just looked at her attire and nodded.

'Got your dark glasses?'

'They—they're in my pocket. My gloves are there too.'

'Then let's go.' He didn't touch her, didn't take her arm and they walked out into bright sunlight on the snow and left the house behind.

It all started again when Cal and a couple of the men went to bring the helicopter out.

'Tony says you're both going tomorrow,' Frank muttered as he came up. 'What's it all about? He's not going to that university until after next summer.'

'There's a lot to do before then, Frank,' Laura said with a bright look kept firmly on her face. 'For one thing, we've got to get a house.'

'Seems to me you've got a house right there,' Frank grumbled, pointing up the slope to the ranch house. 'You've got a job and everything.'

'Oh, Frank, it's not *our* house,' Laura protested. 'We're going home.'

'You called the Bar W home when you fell off that horse and knocked yourself dizzy,' Frank argued. 'Mike said Cal would have brought you back home even if he had to wade through snowdrifts to do it.'

Laura looked frantically at Mike when he came to join

them. He gazed into her eyes as if she were one of his beloved horses and clapped his hand on Frank's shoulder.

'Leave it, Frank,' he said quietly. 'Laura knows what she has to do.'

'She's got to stay here, that's what she's got to do,' Frank grumbled as he went off. Mike looked at Laura and saw far too much. He saw the tears at the back of her eyes and the wild look on her face.

'Going up in the chopper with Cal?' he asked, and when she just nodded he added, 'Enjoy a last look round, then. Don't take Frank's scolding to heart. He's fond of you and Tony. He'll have nobody to mother when you've gone. He'll forget to be grumpy tomorrow.'

Laura gave him a grateful look and went out to where Cal was waiting by the helicopter, Frank's words ringing round her head. Cal would have brought her back if he'd had to wade through snowdrifts. Another thing that Cal had always been willing to do for her and it didn't seem at all like exaggeration.

Cal put her into her seat and was just getting in himself when Tony came haring out of his quarters and skidded to a halt beside the helicopter.

'Can I go up with you?' he asked eagerly. 'I've never had a spin in one of these things. Can I come?'

Cal looked at him for a minute and then said very reasonably, 'No.' He just got in himself and started the engine, then they were lifting smoothly off the ground.

Laura looked down and saw Tony looking upwards with surprise etched all over his face. Mike was with him and he was grinning widely. When she glanced at Cal his face was utterly impassive and she didn't need to ask why he had left Tony behind, he told her.

'This is just for you, Laura. You asked to go up and look around the ranch, so here we are, doing it.'

'You didn't have to,' Laura muttered.

'I have to do anything you ask. Haven't I always? Tomorrow I'm taking you to the train in Leviston and seeing you go. I'm doing that because you want to go.'

Laura started to answer, to tell him that she didn't want to go, but she closed her lips and kept the protest inside. Cal was indulgent but he didn't love her as she loved him. The men on the ranch liked her, but only Tony needed her.

She put on her dark glasses against the white desert of snow and they skimmed over the ranch, giving her a last look at everything she had grown to love. From up here she could see all of it, the trees heavy with snow, the endless prairie wrapped in white and the Rocky Mountains that looked so invincible.

Cal finally flew up into the mountains, letting her see places she had never seen before, and she looked down at deer, running for cover as the noise of the helicopter drove them along. They were lifting their legs high to clear the thick snow, wading across glittering streams and then leaping onto the banks of snow at the other side. Up here, the trees were laden with white, the pine trees looking like a Christmas card.

She saw the lakes where her father had fished with his friend Josh. Now they were covered in ice that gleamed in the sun. There was water, running silent from up here, sparkling in the bright sunlight. She could imagine everything as her father had seen it. She would never have the chance again.

When they eventually flew over the ranch house and settled towards the ground by the sheds, Laura turned to Cal. He had not spoken all the time they had been out and she knew why. He had been giving her a last gift, allowing her to see the place she would always yearn for.

'Thank you,' she told him quietly. 'I'll never forget that.'

'Neither will I,' he said softly. 'You earned it, Laura. It's for the joy you've given to all of us, for your sweet, beautiful face, for your unruly temper and for the way you were soft and eager in my arms, giving me everything. I won't forget it either. How could I?'

When they landed, Laura jumped out before he could come to help her. Before the blades had stopped she was ducking down and running for the ranch house, everything inside her hurting.

Biddy put on a splendid dinner that night and Tony came for the last time. To her surprise, Frank and Mike had also been invited and now Frank did not scold her. He was cheerful and happy, joking with Tony and asking about his university.

'We've got a few universities of our own,' he pointed out wryly. 'You could go there instead of tracking all the way back to England.'

It was a small jab at them for leaving but Tony wasn't upset as Laura felt.

'I'm going to Oxford,' he said. 'It's an ambition I always had. It's very special there with all the spires and all the people who've gone before.'

'You're going to be one of those folks in funny hats and black gowns?' Frank asked.

'If I'm lucky,' Tony laughed.

'Well, don't go playing cards or they'll throw you out,' Mike warned. 'Will you be coming back to visit us, Tiger?'

'I hope so,' Tony said happily. 'I'll never forget this place.'

Laura looked up and met Cal's eyes but she couldn't hold his gaze because she knew that she would never come back to the ranch. Cal would be here and one day he would marry. Facing him then was something she could never do.

Biddy, who had been having this last meal with them,

suddenly disappeared from the table, and when she came back in she had a cake with one candle on the top.

'This is because you're going,' she said. 'I planned it for when you went after a year, so that's why it's got one candle. You're going sooner but it's still got one candle anyhow.'

Laura didn't know what to say and she fought back tears that tried to surface. It was just one more thing to show how much they had meant to the people here and she felt that she was letting them down.

Tony just looked at her and took over, demanding to cut the cake himself, and when there was no more attention on her Laura glanced up at Biddy's face and found that, like her, Biddy was struggling with tears.

'Thank you,' Laura said quietly. 'Thank you for everything, Biddy. You've made me feel so comfortable here in this house.'

Biddy blinked her eyes vigorously. 'You fit in here. You've not been any trouble. You were no trouble even when you were hurt. I could keep on looking after you until I got really old.'

'I don't think you'll ever be really old.' Laura smiled.

'Well, I'm working on it.'

When they all left for the night, Mike lingered and caught Laura just as she was about to escape up to her room. His hand was closed around a silver chain and, when he let her see, it was a chain holding a silver medallion.

'This is for you, Laura. I've had it since I was a boy. It's from my own people and it will bring you good luck.'

Laura stood transfixed as he put it into her hand and then she looked up into the night-black eyes.

'I can't take this, Mike. It's yours.'

'It's yours now. I want to give it to you. It's not something that's sold outside the tribe, so it's special. Wear it round your neck and it will bring good luck always.'

Laura ran her fingers over the delicate working on the medallion. There were words entwined with the pattern but she couldn't read them. 'It's beautiful. What do the words say?'

'They say, "Heart's Desire". All you ever wish for.'

When Laura looked up the dark eyes held her for a second and they were calming, healing, as if he knew something she would never know herself.

'Cal is my brother,' he said quietly. 'He needs one of these as well but I only have this one.'

He turned and went out and Laura fled up to her room, clutching the bright silver in her hand. If only she could have her heart's desire. She knew without thought what it would be, but no silver charm would bring it.

Next morning there was no sun shining. The air was colder still and Laura knew that they were just escaping before a heavy fall made it impossible to leave for days. She had not seen Cal since last night's dinner and now she would have to face him for the last time.

She showered and dressed for travelling before packing her things, but there was none of the excitement she had felt when they'd been coming here. Cal would take them to the train and then they would be gone out of his life, away from the ranch, away from the country and back to England.

At the last minute she picked up the silver charm Mike had given her. She put it around her neck and looked at herself in the mirror. It looked so bright, like a signal, and she couldn't let Cal see it, so she let it fall beneath her sweater and hang between her breasts, nestling secretly against her warm skin. 'Heart's Desire'. If she could have what her heart desired she would only wish for Cal.

He wasn't there for breakfast and he didn't come up to the house at all as the time for going drew closer. Tony came up to carry her things out to the car and, now that they were actually going, he didn't look too pleased either.

Laura was travelling in trousers and her heavy jacket that Cal had bought. She had given some consideration to leaving it behind but it meant too much to her. All the things he had said were running round in her mind. 'Let me buy you things, care for you, make you happy.'

He had done that. He *had* made her happy. Because of Cal, all her bitterness had gone, Tony's too. She had been secure for the first time in her life and it wasn't Cal's fault that she felt like this now. Even the way he had made love to her and been gentle and warm.

Laura was determined that when he came to take them to the train she would keep her misery inside. She would smile and be cheerful. She would thank him for his kindness and not leave him feeling guilty in any way.

When he came she had already said goodbye to a tearful Biddy. She had promised to write each week and send a postcard from Edmonton and another from London and she was struggling with tears herself. Cal just glanced at her and then drove them from the house and down towards the road that led to town.

'Did you say goodbye to your friends?' He looked in the mirror at Tony, who was sitting silently in the back.

'Sure. They seemed sorry to see me go,' Tony murmured gloomily, looking out of the window for one last glimpse of the Bar W. 'I learned a lot here. I've never had so many good friends.'

Laura stared from the window too. She kept her lips tightly closed and willed herself to be calm, to face this separation without tears. But all the same, she couldn't talk cheerfully in spite of her decision earlier. Being wrenched from happiness hurt too much.

Cal didn't say a word to her and Laura asked herself if he had spoken to her at all since the ride in the helicopter. He didn't seem to have even looked at her since then. He didn't look at her now. He was taking them to catch the train and that was all, giving her the freedom to leave everything she loved, and he had timed it so that there would be no hanging around.

The bitter weather had hit Leviston and it was cold by the train. The wind was blowing harshly from the mountains, lingering leaves swirling along the tracks, driven by the devil's knives that were thrown from the Rockies.

Laura snuggled inside her jacket as they hurried along to reach their seats. She knew Cal would not come closer to see them off and she stopped and turned to him as Tony went ahead and began to load their luggage into the train.

Cal was standing impassively, apparently untouched by the bitter cold, just looking at her.

'Thank you,' she said quietly. 'Thank you for everything you've done for us, for the happiness you've given us.' She bit her lips together to hold back tears. 'Thank you for being who you are, for—for being wonderful.'

The hard wind was swirling her hair around her face and she couldn't say anything else without weeping on his shoulder. She was determined not to do that. She turned and hurried off to join Tony as he lifted the last of their luggage aboard.

'Laura!' At the sound of Cal's voice, urgent and deep, Laura turned and looked back at him. He hadn't moved even a step in her direction. He just stood with his hands deep in the pockets of his sheepskin jacket, the wind blowing his black hair and his eyes as brilliantly blue as the sky in summer.

She looked at him helplessly, loving everything about him, getting one long, last look at him.

'Come back home with me,' he said softly. 'Don't go, because I'll only leave the ranch and follow you. I know Tony needs you but I need you too. I love you.'

She stared at him, not quite believing what she heard, her eyes searching his face with a desperation that made him smile slowly.

'I love you, Laura,' he said again, not moving further. 'What else can I say? Go and I'll follow. Come back and I'll cherish you all my life.'

He took his hands from his pockets and held his arms out towards her. Tears were suddenly streaming down her face and Laura ran. She ran right into his arms, sobbing his name, and he lifted her close, his face against her hair.

'Did you imagine for one moment that I could let you go? Did you think I could simply allow you to leave me? Everything would fall apart without you, my love.' He raised her head and smiled into her tear-wet eyes. 'Sure you knew,' he whispered. 'How could you not know? I couldn't keep away from you. I was so desperate to make you mine.'

'You were letting me go,' she choked, looking up into his face.

'I've been fighting my conscience for two days but it didn't stand much of a chance. I'm a lot bigger, so, naturally, I won.' He opened his jacket and brought her inside to his warmth. 'You're cold, sweetheart. Let's get you back to the ranch and Biddy's hot coffee.'

Tony stuck his head out of the train.

'Laura, come on. The train will be leaving,' he shouted.

'Get the luggage off, then, or I'll have the trouble of finding it later,' Cal shouted back. 'We're going home.'

Tony looked at Laura, snuggled against Cal, her arms tightly round his waist, and he started unloading their things. 'Now you tell me,' he grumbled, grinning all over his face. 'You going to help me with this luggage or what?'

'No,' Cal said. 'I don't aim to move from right where I am. Hurry up, though. It's damned cold here.'

Laura didn't even turn to look at her brother. She was smiling, breathing in the scent of the man who held her close, feeling the strong arms around her.

'I love you, Cal,' she whispered.

'I know. Everything shows on your beautiful face. All your hopes, all your fears, all your worries, the way you're pulled in two directions. I thought I could let you go but I couldn't. I could hear you crying inside, struggling with duty.' He dropped a quick kiss on her lips. 'We'll work something out. No more worries, sweetheart.'

Then they were going back home. The train pulled out, its lonely sound echoing across the hills, but by then they had turned to the ranch. Everything inside Laura was singing with joy and Tony was sitting in silence, but his face was happy all the same.

'Come up to the house for dinner tonight,' Cal said quietly. 'We've got a lot of things to talk about and we'll get it all set out immediately. I don't want Laura worrying for one more day. You look like moving back to your old room when we get your books across here. You'll never get a thing done with the boys constantly hassling you to teach them cards tricks.'

'Okay, boss.' Tony grinned.

Cal grinned back at him, their eyes meeting in the mirror. 'Oh, I'll be more than the boss soon, Tiger. I'll be related and then watch out.'

Tony was still grinning when they pulled into the yard

to drop him off with his luggage and Mike came out looking surprised but greatly amused to see them.

'What goes off now?' he asked innocently as Cal stepped out for a minute.

'You want to be best man at my wedding, brother? She didn't escape after all.'

'Well, you certainly left everything to the last minute. I've never seen so many long faces around here. Told you so, didn't I?'

'Yeah, you told me,' Cal agreed and Mike bent to smile into the car at Laura.

'It was the charm,' he murmured. 'Are you wearing it?'

'Right next to my heart, Mike,' she whispered back happily.

When Cal got in to drive her up to the house he wanted to know what the whispering had been about and Laura turned her glorious smile on him.

'Mike gave me a necklace last night. It's an old silver charm from his own people. The words say, "Heart's Desire". I'm wearing it today.'

'You didn't need a charm,' Cal told her, bending to kiss her smiling mouth. 'You beguiled me the moment I first saw you.'

When they walked into the house, Biddy was crossing the hall, still drying her eyes on the edge of her apron, and Cal frowned at her.

'You can stop all that,' he ordered. 'I've brought her back home. I'm taking her things upstairs and then we want some coffee. You can help us plan a winter wedding because it's going to be too long to wait for spring coming around.'

Biddy's face lit up and then she grabbed Laura and danced her round the hall, almost taking her breath away. Cal just smiled his indulgent smile and when Laura ran up the stairs after him and went into her room he was putting her suitcases on the bed.

'Are—are we really getting married?' she asked, her eyes filled with stars.

He walked towards her, pulling her into his arms and beginning to kiss her hungrily. 'We are,' he whispered against her lips. 'As soon as we can. But in the meantime, you're sleeping with me, and if I don't get you soon it will drive me mad.' He let his coat fall to the floor and his hands eased her own coat away until he could feel her softness against him. 'Hmm. That's better,' he murmured seductively. 'One long, hard winter with nothing to do but this. When the snow is too deep for Biddy to make it across to the house, I'm going to make love to you in every room, every time I see you. I'll start right now.'

'You ordered coffee,' Laura reminded him breathlessly.

'I thought you looked cold,' he said, smiling into her eyes. 'You don't look so cold now, though.' He turned her to the door, his arm around her waist. 'We'll go down all the same. I'll have to share you for a while, I suppose, but not for long. I'll wait until tonight.'

When Tony came up, they sat in the big room with coffee, Cal close to Laura on the sofa. He was very business-like but Laura just sat smiling, letting him do all the talking. With her hand firmly in Cal's she was drifting high into the sky, not thinking about anything but how happy she felt.

'There's a long winter coming,' Cal told Tony. 'You'll have nothing much to do but read and work ready for university. I'll get your books sent out and then you're to get right down to it.'

'My books are in the store with all our things,' Tony warned.

'That's no problem. I'll have the lot shipped out here.

Laura can pick out what she wants to keep because I reckon this place will need another addition.'

'But it's big enough already,' Laura protested, suddenly coming out of her happy trance.

'Big enough for how many, honey?' Cal murmured seductively. 'In any case,' he added when her face went glowingly pink and Tony laughed, 'I've had one of my better ideas. I'm going to have a swimming pool tacked onto the end of the house. I'll have you swimming in no time and without any mud too. But you,' he said, turning back to Tony, 'are going to work at those books. I don't want my brother-in-law failing at university. There isn't a man on the ranch who won't be interested in your results. Fail and Mike will belt your hide.'

There was another party at dinner and this time there were no signs of sadness. Frank was beaming as if he'd done it all himself and Biddy wanted to talk about the wedding. She had obviously used the time since they had returned to let her mind roam free. She had plenty of grand ideas and Mike looked startled.

'Don't know if I can cope with this best-man thing,' he worried. 'What about Tiger here?'

'Tiger is Laura's brother. He gets to give the bride away. You're *my* brother so you get to be the best man. Biddy's sure to put you through your paces so stop trying to sneak out of it.'

'Biddy,' Laura said, raising her voice above the hilarity of a party atmosphere, 'is going to be my bridesmaid.'

Biddy's face went pink but she looked pleased. 'Do you think I can do it?' Her eyes brightened. 'Gosh. It will mean a new outfit and a new hairdo.' She sighed. 'It's going to take some figuring out. What are we going to wear, Laura?'

'You can talk about that tomorrow,' Cal ordered in a quelling voice. 'This is going to be the fastest wedding on record because if we get a heavier fall of snow it will have to be put off. We're getting married in Leviston at the church.'

Later when they were in Laura's room and the house was quiet around them and all their own again, Laura lay in Cal's arms and asked about the wedding in Leviston.

'Why can't we have it here at the ranch?'

Cal turned her in his arms and stroked her face. 'Because I want everyone to know you're my wife,' he said softly. 'I want everyone to know how lucky I am.'

Laura smiled up into his handsome face. 'I wanted to get married in a church in any case,' she confessed.

'Thought you might.' He looked down at her seriously. 'I'm going to spend the rest of my life seeing that you get everything you want.'

Laura wound her arms around his neck. 'What do you want, Cal?'

He tightened his arms and pulled her on top of him. 'You—I just want you. I suppose I wanted you from the first moment I saw you but I never thought I'd get you. You were everything I'd dreamed of.'

'I thought it would be Felicity,' Laura confessed. 'Mike told me she wanted you.'

'I never wanted her,' Cal muttered. 'I knew who I wanted right from the first.'

'Mike was strange with her,' Laura mused. 'He treated her like an enemy.'

'Hmm,' Cal said and Laura lifted her head and looked at him, her dark, tilted eyes enquiring.

'Go on. Tell me about it,' she ordered.

'Her parents had a small place the other side of Leviston,' he said, after sighing and grinning at her. 'Felicity was a nuisance from being a teenager. She used to come up here to the Bar W and make trouble every chance she got. She thought it would be a good idea to marry me and finally have the two ranches brought together. She had grand plans that included ruling the whole place.'

'Did you consider marrying her?'

'Hell, I did not! I couldn't throw her off the place because her parents are good people, friends of Josh. But when she started slinking round Mike for fun, she had to go because Mike keeps that temper of his but it was beginning to boil. Luckily her parents had grown weary of ranching and wanted to move to Edmonton so she was shipped off out of our lives.'

'Do you still see her when you go to Edmonton?'

'God, no! I call in to see her parents but only when Felicity is at work.'

He pulled her tightly against him and grinned down at her.

'Anything else? I don't want those lovely eyes turning green.' Before Laura could protest he was kissing her hungrily. When she was breathless from his kisses he sighed and rested his head against her bright hair. 'And another thing,' he added. 'I'd like at least three children, just like you. I've never been greedy in my life but now I think I can indulge myself.'

'Tony will be an uncle.'

'So will Mike.' He raised her chin to look into her eyes. 'He's my brother, Laura. We've been together for a long time.'

'I know. He's getting to be a bit like a brother to me too. It will mean we have a big family all around us.'

'Will you like that?' he asked softly.

'Oh, yes, darling. So much happiness, so much joy.'

'Do you think you'll have time for me?' He sounded just a bit anxious and Laura caught his face between her hands.

'I've loved you since I saw you,' she whispered. 'You were standing in the doorway, so tall, so handsome and so kind. I felt a rush of something inside me that I'd never felt before but I never thought I would be here with you now.'

Then suddenly she was lying beneath Cal and his blue eyes were smiling into hers. 'I love you,' he said quietly. 'I'll adore you always.' His lips met hers and soon they were flying above the mountains, above the snow, safe in each other's arms as the whole world stopped turning and their minds were filled with the glitter of stars.

Modern Romance™
...seduction and
passion guaranteed

Tender Romance™
...love affairs that
last a lifetime

Sensual Romance™
...sassy, sexy and
seductive

Blaze Romance™
...the temperature's
rising

Medical Romance™
...medical drama on
the pulse

Historical Romance™
...rich, vivid and
passionate

27 new titles every month.

*With all kinds of Romance for
every kind of mood...*

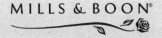

the *Mother's Day* collection

Margaret Way Kate Hoffmann Helen Dickson

Money Off Voucher
see inside for details

Available from 21st February 2003

*Available at most branches of WH Smith,
Tesco, Martins, Borders, Eason, Sainsbury's
and all good paperback bookshops.*

0303/024/MB65

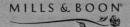

FREE!
2 Books
and a surprise gift!

We would like to take this opportunity to thank you for reading this Mills & Boon® book by offering you the chance to take TWO more specially selected titles from the Tender Romance™ series absolutely FREE! We're also making this offer to introduce you to the benefits of the Reader Service™ —

- ★ FREE home delivery
- ★ FREE gifts and competitions
- ★ FREE monthly Newsletter
- ★ Books available before they're in the shops
- ★ Exclusive Reader Service discount

Accepting these FREE books and gift places you under no obligation to buy; you may cancel at any time, even after receiving your free shipment. Simply complete your details below and return the entire page to the address below. *You don't even need a stamp!*

YES! Please send me 2 free Tender Romance books and a surprise gift. I understand that unless you hear from me, I will receive 4 superb new titles every month for just £2.55 each, postage and packing free. I am under no obligation to purchase any books and may cancel my subscription at any time. The free books and gift will be mine to keep in any case.

N3ZEB

Ms/Mrs/Miss/Mr ....Initials...

BLOCK CAPITALS PLEASE

Surname...

Address...

....

....Postcode ....

Send this whole page to:
UK: The Reader Service, FREEPOST CN81, Croydon, CR9 3WZ
EIRE: The Reader Service, PO Box 4546, Kilcock, County Kildare (stamp required)